ANOTHER

BOOK OF

MORMONS

PAUL RAYMOND REID

This is a work of fiction. All of the characters, organizations, and events portrayed in this novel are either products of the author's imagination or are used fictitiously.

ANOTHER BOOK OF MORMONS.
Copyright © 2019 by Paul Raymond Reid. All rights reserved.

The scanning, uploading, and distribution of this book without permission is a theft of the author's intellectual property. If you would like to use material from the book (other than for review purposes), please contact author via www.paulraymondreid.com.

Printed in the United States of America.
ISBN: 9781489511324

Dedication art by Lennie Alickman

Cover design by Justin Burks
Book design by Limpede Ink

To our two dearly departed Welsh Corgis, Magda and Vickers,

who taught us so much about authenticity and steadfastness.

ANOTHER BOOK OF MORMONS

PAUL RAYMOND REID

I have had to write and rewrite this book countless times in order to forge a book worthy of the Sisterdom and of him, the would-be Prophet. For it was he that found a book that was related to another book. I thought I would be lost in the writing for I am writing about that which was lost, then found, then lost again forever. I could only make sense of it by focusing on his wives in their Sisterdom, to think as they might have thought. I had to include the testimony of each in their turn, for they are the tellers, the commenters, the testifiers. Hearing and rendering their voices allowed me to think of their roles and their Mormon pasts, and that of the Prophet. For only then could I make a certain sense of the Prophet's tale. The Sisterdom is my lifeline. It is only in them that I have gained any solace.

—Eugene Lannon

CHAPTER ONE

Eugene Lannon

JULY 4, 1862
SALT LAKE CITY OPERA HOUSE

I approached the podium guarded by three matched protectors and asked the middle of these Mormons for President Young.

The sentinel eyed me skeptically. "The Prophet Brigham be up there." He gestured to two Elders engaged in a heated discussion, oblivious to the day's festivities that were about to begin.

The rightmost had to be the Prophet. There was a stunning sharpness to his sun-burnt leanness. He was tall, over six feet, with deep-set seer's eyes. A vigorous man in his mid-fifties. He had a patrician nose, etched cheekbones, and a healthy head of gray hair, curled at the ears, set off by bushy, black eyebrows. He was ordering the other Elder about with the ingrained power of a Prophet. I heard clearly only one word the seer declaimed, "Twelve."

The leftmost had to be his underling. Unlike the severely dark-suited diviner, the subordinate was very plainly dressed for this celebratory day in the thinnest of gray, homespun clothing. He was of no more than medium height, and though broad-shouldered, was portly for a Mormon. His face was smooth except for reddish-gray whiskers. His similarly hued hair produced thick, comical curls atop his head. He smiled through calm, gray-blue eyes at the gesticulating Prophet like a steady lead carpenter taking orders from a difficult client. He laughed off the other's remonstrance as if enjoying some particular jest.

I approached the podium stairs but was restrained by the guards.

"Let Mr. Lannon pass," the one I took to be the underling intoned with a placid assuredness.

"Mr. Young, glad to meet you." I offered my hand to the righteous seer but was surprised when the unassuming factotum answered with his extended right hand. So this unprepossessing man was Mormon's Lion of the Lord. How embarrassing.

"I heard tell from your editor you were coming to Deseret. Call me Brother Brigham. And welcome to the Land of the Saints."

I had been sent by my Herald editor, James Gordon Bennett, in answer to a great curiosity about the Mormons and to offer our readers, and myself for that matter, a respite from the depressing news of the Civil War. Bennett, an honorary Brigadier General of the Mormon Legion, had been offered sainthood in heaven by Joseph Smith for his even-handed reporting on this creative religious sect. I had come to Utah to follow up on the Mormon story, to seek it out where it had fled from scrutiny of the press.

"I wanted to place myself at the center of the Mormon faith to report upon it fairly." Bennett had warned me how difficult it was to write fairly of the unique Mormon life—be it fiction or nonfiction. I had pledged to live with and fully engage the sect to understand it. I would not write a travelogue of half-hearted animation but would reflect upon the inner workings of the Mormon religion and families. I would avoid writing another sensational, bigoted, penny dreadful attack on the Mormons. I resolved to tie my tongue, to open my eyes and ears, to learn close-up all I could of their doctrines and practices, and understand for myself the truth or falsehood of the reports I had heard concerning them. Then I would decide what to record and how to author my tale.

"We trust the Herald. You are not one of our enemies who are like a thousand hungry wolves surrounding a solitary lamb. The animals howl and yelp and cry for our blood," Brother Brigham said without anger. "But every time they kick this lamb of Mormonism, they kick it upstairs."

If this be Brigham Young, then who was the prophetic one? Brother Brigham answered my unasked question by turning to introduce the tall, lean, prepossessing man. "Bishop John Sweet of Cache County. Patriarch Sweet manages our rural stake north of the city and is our emissary to the Shoshone Indians." Patriarch Sweet—for he did remind me most of some Biblical Patriarch—waved off my offered hand dismissively. I felt rejected.

"Like the Book teaches us, the Shoshone are of the chosen seed of Abraham," Patriarch Sweet said with a preacher's definitiveness.

"The Indians are our charge. We must feed them and clothe them and teach them the stable arts of husbandry," Brother Brigham added.

"I have mastered their language so that I can convert them to the Mormon way," the Patriarch summed up his ultimate mission.

"Now that Colonel Connor's troops have taught 'em a lesson and the Shoshone are no longer deadly to whites," Brother Brigham said.

Perhaps this was my opening. I aimed my thoughts at Brother

Brigham as arbiter. "I would like to report on a different side of the Mormons. I would like to see a Mormon family up-close, away from Salt Lake City. We Easterners need a fresh take on Mormons. I hope to get inside a polygamist family. To learn how it was formed and how it works. A painter, Abel Bermann, has joined my wife and me, and he wants to paint Mormons, the countryside, the mountains, and the Indians."

I looked out into the seated audience where Abel and my wife, Abigail, as was their want, were sitting close to each other. I had not wanted to bring Abigail to Utah, but she had pled directly with Abel that she be included. And since Abel was the source of some of the funds for our trip, Abigail came along.

"I trust you are finding your accommodation at the Salt Lake City Hotel acceptable," Brother Brigham said.

Did the Mormon leader know everything? I had heard that Brother Brigham had a network of informers. Had he spies everywhere, even at our hotel?

"Come to Cache Valley. I will host you there." Patriarch Sweet's offer had the sound of a command. "There you can see my wives and family at work and find colorful mountain landscapes and striking Shoshone ready for painting. I will have each of my wives tell their story." I found promise in the Patriarch's offer, particularly his plural wives. They would show me the inner workings of polygamy.

Brother Brigham paused like an accountant toting up the ledger. He turned to one of the three guards and ordered, "Fetch Brother Port."

The guard returned quickly with a barrel-chested gladiator of a man with long, unkempt hair. His face had a massive lower jaw. His firm mouth befit a mastiff.

"Brother Port Rockwell." Brigham placed his right hand on Port's strongly made, broad shoulders. "He will travel with you to Cache Valley... to help you with your research." Patriarch Sweet eyed Brother Port doubtfully. Port looked me over with a scowl. I assumed that Port was assigned to our group to monitor what a Gentile journalist was about.

The festivities' start was heralded as the band began what I assumed was the unofficial national anthem. We all left the podium. I sang along to this awkward tune haltingly but was confused, as the Saints bellowed out a differing set of words. I listened closely to catch this revised Mormon text.

Its guardians are sending their ministers forth
To tell when the Latter Day Kingdom is founded
And invite all the lovers of truth on the earth
Jew, Christian, and Gentile, to gather around it;
The cause will prevail, though all else may assail,
For God has decreed that his works shall not fail;
Oh! The ensign of Israel's streaming abroad,
And ever shall wave o'er the people of God.

Although Brother Brigham carried the unwieldy tune well, Patriarch Sweet's basso voice dominated the ensemble.

I returned to my seat. Abigail and Abel chatted away as the prayers and sermons began. Brother Brigham gave a brief speech chock-full of planting information and crop yields. It was oddly uninspiring.

I took in this place of public amusement that for beauty and comfort rivaled my much-missed New York Academy of Music. The Mormon Opera House sat 2,500 and had been expanded to receive five hundred more by covering the stage to accommodate dancing. My greatest surprise was at the exquisite artistic beauty of the gilded arch over the stage.

Abigail sneered at the dress of the Mormon folk. Few men wore patrician broadcloth and silk. Most menfolk made do with plebeian tweed. Some ladies sported jewelry or feathers. But most were in the poorest of calico dresses. There were some pretty girls festive in puffed tarlatans. I sighted Patriarch Sweet, who had joined his plurality of women. The oldest was the more elaborately dressed as she chaperoned what I took to be the younger wives. I counted them as eight.

The talking ceased and a tall, firm-figured, brown-haired beauty approached Brother Brigham. I heard her name, "Sister Amelia", whispered through the crowd. She led Brother Brigham up onto the stage to commence the dancing. The orchestra began an old-fashioned contra-dance worthy of the days of Mozart. I was much impressed by the aristocratic grace with which Brother Brigham and Sister Amelia danced.

I glanced over at the Patriarch, my assigned host. He sat bolt upright. He would not dance, nor would his more spiritual wives. He ignored the display Brother Brigham made. I sensed that he did not approve of this unseemly regalia. I would go to Cache Valley to study up-close the Patriarch and his true Mormon family.

CHAPTER ONE

JULY 5, 1862
CACHE VALLEY

Abigail, Abel, and I woke early for our trip to Cache Valley. Abel, for once not knocking knees with my wife, would ride in the first of two open, mule-pulled Conestoga wagons with the Patriarch and four of his wives. I was introduced to the four wives who rode up front with the Patriarch, but only the name of the first wife, "Mother Evangeline", registered. This austere matriarch looked Abigail over with a distrusting glare.

Our designated guide, Port, rode his game horse beside the Patriarch's wagon. The saw handles of two revolvers peeped through his blouse.

"I ain't much for book larnin' and I can't help ya writ nuthin'," Port had said when we met up, "but I aim I can help you with Brother Sweet and the Injuns."

Abigail and I were assigned the second prairie schooner with the second quartet of the Patriarch's wives. Three benches fronted to the fore with their leather cushions and hinged padded backs. After the uncomfortable ride on our overland stagecoach west, minus Abel for once, Abigail and I settled snugly into the rear seat.

"It's so good to see someone from back east. We do get a bit isolated in the Valley." Sister Katherine, who sat in front of us, turned graciously to make conversation with the innate calmness of a contemplative woman. "I am Sister Katherine, the singer, the second of Patriarch Sweet's wives."

Her seatmate, Sister Willa, hugely pregnant, giggled, "And I am Sister Willa, the sixth." Abigail looked with alarm at the Sister's about-to-pop belly. Abigail was never one to think too highly of child-birthing. Thankfully the labors of our marriage had not tested her.

The occupants of the first bench did not chime in, so Sister Katherine reintroduced them. "That is Sister Sarah, the eighth wife." The dark-hued, mere slip of a girl acknowledged us with a smile-less face. "And Sister Nona, the fourth wife." I had noticed the withdrawn nature of Sister Nona when we were first introduced by the Patriarch, so I was not surprised when she failed to turn in response. She cast her eyes downward. She was not much for pleasantries.

"We are the bedmates of the Blue Room. Not the select of the Gold Room," Sister Katherine said with quiet humor in her voice.

"Blue Room? Gold Room? I'm afraid I don't understand," I queried.

"Besides the children's rooms, we have three bedrooms in Patriarch Sweet's house. The Gold Room is where Mother Evangeline and the sealed wives sleep, most of whom have given the Patriarch living sons. And then there is the Blue Room where the rest of us sleep. Plus the Patriarch's own bedroom, of course," Sister Katherine explicated for us Gentiles whimsically. I filed away this introduction as something worthy of further research.

Bedrooms full of wives, full of interlocking personal history.

The tilting of the two vehicles was a bit ominous. The road was passable but hardly smoothened. Wives clung to their seats so as not to be tossed.

The well-watered Valley invited us as it shimmered in the obscuring summer heat. This rich, open, remote valley, surrounded

CHAPTER ONE

by imposing hills, was a world away from linear Salt Lake City. The Valley charmed but threatened with a too bright green tapestry of flowering grass, willow copses, and long lines of aspen, beech, and cottonwood. I was sure that Abel, our painter, was up front planning an unrepeatable play of obvious, garish colors. I cautioned myself not to lose focus on the worthy story of a Mormon family in the deceiving beauties of the Valley's landscape. Despite the warmth of the day—it was over ninety degrees in the coach—Abigail and the four Mormon Sisters did not sweat so dry was the air.

"We are entering Sweetville," Sister Willa hailed her surroundings with pride in her voice.

Village gardens, plentiful orchards, graceful poplars, dark, rich alfalfa fields—Sweetville was an idyll. Farmers, who were guarded by men with rifles, plowed an earth made tawny by maize and corn. Numberless red, black, and white-dotted cattle and horses speckled the sage. So this was the goodly land where souls came to be satisfied?

We entered the village proper, laid out on a standard Mormon plan. All dwellings were in blocks, eight lots to a block, blocks separated by wide streets. The houses were of adobe. Adobe was used for its warmth, insulation, and security. The houses faced each other so that a block could be cordoned off to provide the safety of a fort against the Shoshone.

I was immediately struck by the soothing sound of running water. Each block had a five-foot-wide ditch alongside to carry household water. The water lulled the senses. But I as a writer must be perceptive.

Sister Katherine explained the abundance of water: "The

nearby, ample Sweetville Creek flows westward into the mighty Bear River."

We were shown the Patriarch's house, which was set apart from the fort-like village.

Again Sister Katherine explained, "The Patriarch wanted a stone house. He hired a mason who was working on the Logan Tabernacle to build him a house fit for a Bishop."

Though we would not see its inside that day, I noted how the house lorded over Sweetville. Therein must lie the Blue Room and the Gold Room.

The wagons stopped at the Bishop's house to discharge the Patriarch and his wives. Our wagon doubled back into the village grid to drop Abigail, Abel, and me off at a more typical, one-story adobe dwelling allotted to writers and painters.

I tried to satisfy Abigail that evening but could not focus on her. My manhood would not suffice. All I thought about was the manliness of the Patriarch with his eight wives. What was he doing this evening with his Sisterdom? Abigail got up after an hour of my flailing efforts to please, flinging the cover from our bed to the floor and stomping out to the central room. I regained my sleep and dreamed uneasily of a beast hidden within the female form, a female rooster ready to play the man. Was this Abigail or one of the Patriarch's wives?

Tomorrow I was to begin my interviews of the Patriarch's wives, to find what had driven each into this web of Sisterdom. I then would weave together a story, perhaps for the Herald, perhaps as my fictional debut. I, who could not properly manage my one wife, must try to understand eight.

CHAPTER TWO

The Testimony of Sister Sarah, the Eighth Wife

JULY 6, 1862
SWEETVILLE

I must stop my dreaming of the free Shoshone world outside. I must get up now to do my Mormon duties. Up, up, they say. Raise yourself up. Lighten the Lamanite load. I must not show them that I still fight their ways. I will not let them see that my growing stomach is sour, as sour as the Patriarch himself.

Sister Katherine, my teacher, would be proud of me, her prize student. With her help I can speak, sing, write, even think in English, though my thoughts often relapse to Shoshone. "We teach you the higher Mormon ways." Why must I be taught Mormon ways? Are they better than Shoshone?

I, White Cloud, am now called Sister Sarah. For that is the accursed name that the Patriarch has forced upon me. I am wed on orders from my Shoshone father. Our leader says the Shoshone must learn to accommodate. The Patriarch had been sent to minister to the Shoshone, to learn our language in order to trick us, to steal our streams and valleys, to save us from our violent ways. Brother Brigham had commanded token Mormons to take a Lamanite wife from among us. For was not marriage the strongest tie of friendship that could exist? So was it not fitting that the Patriarch might take me, the daughter of Chief Sagwitch, the daughter rightfully known as White Cloud, as his eighth wife? The Patriarch makes me into Sister Sarah. It is the Mormon plan to raise me up white and delightsome. Up from the darkness of barbarity into the whiteness of civilization.

At least the Patriarch will not bid me come to his bedroom for my complete term. I can even nurse this accursed babe, whatever it be, in peace. He will not force me back into his bedroom too early, lest his attentions entail upon his offspring un-holy desires and appetites.

Before, in those darker early days, whenever I had been summoned to the Patriarch's bedroom after dinner—it happened with fortnightly regularity—I was not treated promiscuously. I was laid down upon his bed without embrace, with a minimum of barely tolerated touch. The Patriarch dutifully spilled his seed within me and then bid me return to the safety of the Blue Room. The Patriarch had done upon me his assigned duty: to amalgamate, to take me down, to populate the earth, hopefully with sons. I dread that this burden be a son.

I listen to Sister Katherine. I hear her sing softly the noble Mormon songs. I try to accept the Mormon stories as yet another set of tales of the Great Spirit, but cannot. I have been received into the Mormon Sisterdom, but I remain a Shoshone. I still dream of fleeing the house of Patriarch Sweet to return to my tribe, but my tribe has abandoned me. I am no longer a full Shoshone. I am part of Chief Sagwitch's plans to forge ties with the Mormons against the Federal army. I must comply and stay put. I have lost my proud

CHAPTER TWO

Shoshone name, White Cloud, and been sentenced to my new name of Sister Sarah. I must remain in Sweetville.

I only feel safe in the physical closeness of the Blue Room with Sisters Willa and Katherine. I share a bed on rotating nights with three Sisters: first Sister Willa, then Sister Katherine, then Sister Nona. I prefer the physical closeness of my nights in one of the two narrow beds spooned to Sister Willa, also with child and farther advanced in term, or in the arms of the more elderly, benign, but ill, Sister Katherine. With the moody Sister Nona it is more difficult. Though we sleep closely together, I can neither give nor find solace. She is the Sister who always pulls away.

Sister Willa and Sister Katherine try to make a pet of me, to tutor me in the proper role of a Mormon wife. Under their tutelage, my English, this language that I must speak, has indeed improved. I talk and write as a white Sister. I even laugh again haltingly. All in the Blue Room laugh—except Sister Nona, who is sentenced to remain ever silent, watchful, and dour. I do laugh, but my laughter remains Shoshone.

My marriage is an abomination. I find some respite in the closeness of Sisterdom with Sisters Willa and Katherine. Whether we three talk together or are silent, we are safe in a Blue Room affinity that triumphs over anything the Patriarch might do and anything those Sisters of the Gold Room might dictate. Willa, Katherine, and I gaze at each other through the prism of our burden, this shared husband, and without need of any gross, unbridled passion, find within each other the shelter of a truer three-pronged marriage.

I can still look proudly in the mirror at my glistening white teeth and comb out my sleek, long, black hair. I can still show that I am Shoshone. I can proudly descend into the kitchen and face the Gold Room wives, the other, less welcoming four of my Sisters in Christ.

I meet Sister Karita first, her blond, Danish coolness ever comely, ever remote. Sister Karita has her two-year-old, golden-haired babe, Alexander, proudly at her side. She never pays any mind to me, Sister Sarah, a mere Shoshone from the Blue Room. I am quick to return her indifference. At her older son Joseph's birth and survival, Patriarch Sweet had commanded that Sister Karita and he be sealed properly in the far off capital, Salt Lake City. With Joseph's survival, Karita has graduated into the more exalted bedroom, the Gold Room. She is welcome to it.

I next see Sister Prudence, that wizened, barren, would-be poetess. Although she is without offspring, Sister Prudence is elevated to the Gold Room by her ties to the Prophet Joseph Smith. She had been sealed proudly and properly to her first husband, the Prophet, before his murder. Of course she warranted the Gold Room. Let her stay there.

Sister Prudence is always peering at my black eyes in search of something deep and hidden. At least today Sister Prudence does not deign to call me "snaky and mistrustful" or harp on "the proper blessings of Mormon civilization" or tell me to "pay proper mind to the truth of the Patriarch's Prophecy." Sister Prudence sits in the corner quietly with her assembled papers, scribbling and revising. Sister Prudence is a true Mormon: writing it all down as the Lord hath commanded, setting great store by her daily journals and ill-constructed poetry. Events, be they noteworthy or not, must be recorded and preserved. If she were to lose her papers, she would

CHAPTER TWO

be helpless. I have learned to pay no mind to the self-proclaimed authoress. I pass by her without greeting or acknowledgement.

Next to enter the kitchen is Sister Hannah. "My son, Evan, will join us tonight for dinner. He wants to meet the writer folk and the painter," she announces with pride to the assembled Sisterdom. She looks over my growing stomach doubtfully. She would never accept a half-breed Lamanite as a proper son. It was after the birth of her eldest living son that the Patriarch—experimenting as he would with Mormon doctrine—had decided that he would henceforth only be sealed to those of his wives who provided him properly with sons who lived past the age of one. As the blessed mother of two sons, including the Patriarch's eldest son, Brother Evan—who lives alone upriver in the community grist mill—Sister Hannah has earned her proper occupancy in the Gold Room. I am quite happy to sleep in a bedroom apart from Sister Hannah's haughtiness.

Seated at the head of the kitchen table, ever-watching, is Mother Evangeline. She is the head wife of our Sisterdom. As first wife she dictates. Although Mother Evangeline has no living sons and does not know how to act maternal, she, who once had a son, had been previously sealed to the Patriarch before he began his experiments with Mormon doctrine. Of course she is given the precedence of an uneasy rest in the larger Gold Room.

Mother Evangeline looks up as I enter the kitchen. She checks me out to see that I am properly subservient. I fail. I am not meek enough to receive from my betters my proper assignments. Despite her leadership, Mother Evangeline does not try to hide her contempt for me, this Lamanite girl with dark skin and degenerate status. How the Patriarch has lowered the family by adding a Shoshone as his eighth wife!

"You must go out in search of wild herbs today, Sister Sarah," Mother Evangeline says slowly as if lecturing a simpleton. "We need more Mormon tea, and some mushrooms, and if you can find it, we need some spotted cowbane poison for the rats. Be sure to place them in their proper spots in the rack." Mother Evangeline gestures to an open square rack on the wall with nine, three-inch square compartments across and nine down. I know what I must find, how to allot it for its proper usage. I, properly trained by Shoshone women, am at home in the forest. I can find the astringent herbs that would dress wounds. I can locate the leaves of the white willow that act as an emetic. I know which mushrooms to harvest and which to leave alone. I can find the poisoned roots to control vermin.

"I will go out this afternoon in search of what you ask," I reply. Let loose from the Patriarch's house, I will try to meet up with my Shoshone brother, Twin Spirit.

The Patriarch enters the kitchen and we eight wives sit down to receive our morning instruction. After a brief prayer, he begins to talk about our guests, the Lannons and the painter. "We must show them the strengths and blessings of spiritual wifehood. Pay particular attention to the writer, Lannon. Tell him much, but be careful what you say. We must convince him that ours is the superior way."

After a quick meal, the Patriarch dismisses the eight of us with a perfunctory nod. He catches me before I can move safely away. "It is a blessing to see you in eternal increase continuing my seed. I foresee that the child will be a son in all his Celestial glory."

"Must I move to the Gold Room then? I am happy where I am." I will not be penned up there. May my child be female, another child for the true Sisters to raise, one I could nurse safely away from the Patriarch's advances. If the child were a male, perhaps he might yet die quickly.

"When you have weaned my son and returned to my bed, the curse of your Lamanite color shall be at last removed." I try to get away from the Patriarch, but he restrains me by grabbing my arm forcefully. "The last traces of White Cloud will be eradicated. I will have more power to protect your Shoshone brethren from the Federal troops. With our Mormon shield guaranteed, no Bear River Massacre will ever take place again."

JANUARY 29, 1862
BEAR RIVER

What do I remember seeing, remember being told by Twin Spirit or by my father, Chief Sagwitch, remember by imagining what might have been? The past was so close to me, but still, though I tell it to myself and to journalists, I have difficulty keeping it in focus.

I rose before first light and wrestled awake Twin Spirit from one of his prophetic dreams. It was early to leave our wickiup, one of the remaining forty tents in our Shoshone camp. Our family teepee was made of sixteen skins tied together with sinews. We had to leave its warmth behind. It was bone-chilling cold outside but we felt liberated.

We climbed quickly out of the willow-full depression that hosted winter quarters on Kuiyapa, the Bear River. Our two eager faces were flush with the warming steam of the nearby hot springs.

We were two happy Shoshone off exploring.

It had only been a few weeks since our Shoshone tribe had gathered for the Warm Dance. Twin Spirit, my sacred brother/sister, had led the thousands of the tribe in the sacred ritual certain to drive out the cold and bring forth the warmth of spring. I had won the winter foot race—how that had angered the warriors.

The night of the Warm Dance, Twin Spirit had a dream where he foretold that some calamity was about to take place. He pled with our father, Chief Sagwitch, to move the Shoshone out of the area.

"Death will come, always out of season," Chief Sagwitch replied. "It is the command that each must face alone. We must obey." Chief Sagwitch asked Twin Spirit to make strong medicine so that they might triumph over the pony soldiers and gain many scalps and horses. When other parts of the Shoshone tribe had left, only our small group led by our father, Chief Sagwitch, remained near the Kuiyapa.

Chief Sagwitch, our sage father, awoke as we, his two children left the wickiup. He nodded as we climbed to the safety of the hill to the west.

As he told us later, his eyes peered through the steaming mist eastward, looking for movement. He sighted some but did not panic. So they had finally come, he thought, the Federal troops from Camp Douglas sent to watch over, protect the Mormons, and teach the Shoshone yet another lesson. The tribe's allotted time had come.

He went from wickiup to wickiup waking each family calmly in turn. To those warriors who seemed overeager to fight, he motioned for quiet and quick preparation. Hopefully the Federal contingent would not be too large and they could be bargained with. Perhaps their leader would show wisdom and merely ask for those warriors who had been falsely accused of stealing Mormon cattle and leave with a token few. That was what I imagined might have happened, for Sagwitch was wise.

Our one hundred warriors made ready. Each gathered his long, black hair with a scarlet cloth into a plait on the side of his head. Each adorned his braided scalp-lock with a strip of otter skin. Each donned their porcupine-quilled, deerskin shirt fringed with dyed horsehair. Each added a white blanket. Each armed himself with bow and arrow, tomahawk, and scalping knife. Too few were allotted the rifles kept hidden by woven willow pads. The warriors were set to meet the Great Spirit face-on if that was his will. For the Great Spirit knew when battles were due and who should win or lose.

Chief Sagwitch was unsure whether we had the forces for victory. The tribes were lodged in a fortifiable ravine three-quarters of a mile in length that turned south and opened up into the Bear River. In the area where the fighting might come, the ravine was forty-feet wide with near perpendicular banks. We would survive if the Federal army had not brought too many troops.

Oblivious to any danger, Twin Spirit and I happily ran a foot race through the new fallen snow on the bluff. I pulled ahead. Twin Spirit, burdened by his mixed apparel of brave and squaw's clothing, was no match for me. He tripped trying to catch up with me. Twin Spirit fell forward into the welcoming arms of the unspoiled snow. He accepted defeat with a laugh. He was content to trail a champion runner like me, for such was the dictate of our two fates. I joined him rolling in the snow.

Suddenly Patriarch Sweet, the Mormon leader whose village

was some fifteen miles distant to the east, was by our side. The reluctant Mormon reached down and helped me up. The Patriarch did not touch Twin Spirit. The Patriarch's contempt for Twin Spirit, this abominable dual-sexed Shoshone, showed on his face.

"What ya here fur?" Twin Spirit asked in his fractured English.

"God has told me that there will be a great battle today," the Patriarch answered, peering off in the direction from which we had run.

"Are the Federals goin' 'tack?"

"Just let's wait and see."

Twin Spirit turned to me. "We must return to our wickiup," he said. We were Shoshone and must support the braves in battle.

Twin Spirit bolted away from Patriarch Sweet, who clung fast to my arm. I bit the Mormon as I tried to pry myself loose.

"Let me go, Mormon. I must rejoin my people," I demanded.

"No, you will stay with me," Patriarch Sweet spoke in the Shoshone tongue. "Our Great Spirit has ordained it. Let's move closer. We must witness what God has ordered to happen." The Patriarch held me tight.

We watched as the full force of Federal troops advanced. I recognized their leaders, Port Rockwell, the guide, and Colonel Connor. Port Rockwell was the five-dollar-a-day guide that day for Colonel Connor's augmented forces. A smaller group came first, followed by a much larger. Connor must have wanted the Shoshone to think there was only a small detachment of infantry ready for negotiation, not for fighting. Connor and Port were followed by what I later learned were four cavalry divisions. Forty armory soldiers were in place with their artillery. They had all rendezvoused near the Bear

CHAPTER TWO

River. Connor would wait no longer. It was frostbite cold after the cavalry's night march. Unyielding winds from the slopes of Cache Valley peppered their ghostlike faces.

I heard Connor address his men. "Winter is the best time to catch these guilty scamps. They are camped along the Bear River ready for the taking. We attack now."

"What shall we do with the prisoners?" Port asked Connor.

"We don't anticipate takin' any prisoners." Connor clipped his answer lest his moistened breath bring frost to his lips. "We'll teach these Shoshone a lesson they will not soon forget."

Fear ran through me.

Chief Sagwitch, my father, often recounted how he looked across the ravine at the assembled troops, these toguashes. He, of course, understood at once that this was not some small contingent ready for negotiation. Without hesitation, he mounted his bouncing war pony. He raised his war lance, ready to lead his warriors into battle.

Even though Chief Sagwitch knew their time had come, I heard him shout for my people not to shoot first. He must give the Federal leader his chance to be a just and wise man.

The early rays of morning continued to cut through the smoke of the hot springs. The Shoshone were ready. One Shoshone taunted a group of toguashes, "Come on you Californ' sons of beetches! Attack us if you dare." The Shoshone warriors were confident of victory, for were they not lodged deep in this fortified ravine? Here they could withstand the Federal troops.

I saw Twin Spirit approach the village. The squaws, he later told me, were anxious. Fearing what would happen next, they let out low-pitched moans. Twin Spirit took his natural leadership role over the women, directing them sharply to act in support of the warriors. He helped our grandmother, Que he gup, prepare ointments for those who might be wounded.

Connor had not come to talk. He raised his arm and directed the artillery to commence firing. Barrage after barrage decimated the Shoshone ranks. Tens of warriors and squaws were struck by the cascading fire. I watched each of our remnant fall. Horror was everywhere. I could not pry myself loose from the Mormon.

Too few braves had rifles that could return fire. After softening their resistance, Connor ordered the cavalry to charge by fording the creek. Not all of the cavalry horses were up to the task and a few soldiers were thrown into the icy water.

My father, Chief Sagwitch, led a counter-charge. When there were hand-to-hand battles on either shore, the Federal soldiers with the advantage of pistols and ample ammunition often had the upper hand. But our Shoshone from their entrenched position fought gamely. I tried to be hopeful but could not. Wounded Shoshone attempted to swim across the creek, but the rifleman standing on the east shore picked them off without mercy. The dead braves were swept downstream to an icy and bloody grave. A lucky few clambered up the bluff.

I struggled with Patriarch Sweet. His grasp was too much for me. I bit him again but he stoically ignored my attempts to escape. For him it was God's charge that I see it all.

I watched him, reading his thoughts. He calmly watched the battle unfold below us with satisfaction. The Mormons had suffered enough from these thieving Shoshone. The Mormon men of Sweet-

CHAPTER TWO

ville would not pitch in and help the Federals, but Patriarch Sweet looked on in approval. Breathless with anger, I vowed to get revenge on this sly Mormon.

Connor gave the order to surround the Indian camp from the west to seal off any escape route at the end of the ravine. What had been a battle turned into slaughter. The toguashes attacked from the rear, slaughtering the braves, the squaws, and the children. Many Shoshone were first shot and then axed to death without mercy. Warrior was piled upon warrior. I cried out in despair.

I watched my father, the Chief, tumble into the creek and hide ashore downstream amongst the brush. He would remain there until night had fallen and then gather the surviving braves to flee north.

Twin Spirit later recounted his tale. He was flying around as if there was no ground underneath his feet. He raced to salve the wounded but there were too many. He dashed in and out among the whizzing bullets but was not hit. He was a ma ai'pots, blessed amalgam of he and she, and was naturally protected from death by the Great Spirit. He heard cries of pain and saw death all around. He found our grandmother, Que he gup, standing beside our still unburned wickiup. She feared the soldiers were going to set the teepee on fire at any moment.

She screamed at him, "Let us stay outside and lie amongst the dead." He obeyed. He chanted soundlessly to the Great Spirit. "Keep your eyes closed tightly," Que he gup muttered.

He continued chanting as he lay beside Que he gup. The battle was winding down. Only those braves who fled would survive. He wanted to see what was happening. He opened his eyes. This nearly cost him his life. A soldier came up. He pointed his gun at my blessed brother.

Port Rockwell came along. "Don't waste your ammunition on a squaw. They are not worth the trouble."

Thus, the Great Spirit protected his loyal ma ai'pots. When the freezing toguashes had fled for the day back to their distant camp, he arose.

I, White Cloud, knew the end of the story. The Patriarch let me loose to run to Twin Spirit. The ground was red with blood. The burning wickiups blackened the earth. Wasted brown seeds and nuts were scattered everywhere. Stomped blue and purple, the dried berries colored the soil.

Twin Spirit addressed the survivors, "This be sacred ground. Let dust be blessed by our blood. Ever heed the cries of braves, squaws, and children. Revenge, on the Federals, on the Mormons."

Patriarch Sweet approached and regained a hold on my arm. I would not let any Mormon see me cry. He touched me on the shoulder in an ill-considered attempt at solace. He led me back to Sweetville. "I will talk with your father, Chief Sagwitch, if God has willed that he survive. You belong to me now as my eighth wife."

I told this story to whoever would listen, including nosy writers. I asked Lannon why he wanted to hear my Shoshone tale. Did it signify anything?

"You, who are different," he answered, "highlight what is most Mormon."

CHAPTER TWO

JULY 6, 1862
SWEETVILLE

I enter the forest as a Shoshone in search of herbs, Mormon tea, mushrooms, and poison roots. I quickly find the required herbs and the Mormon tea that Mother Evangeline dotes upon. I place them separately in the compartments of my medicine bag. As I head up Temple Hill, a sacred healing place for our tribe, I am not surprised to hear a clear step through the drowsy hum of the midday forest. I recognize the measured gait of a Shoshone. I know it is Twin Spirit.

My divine, dual-selfed brother darts to my side. He/she wears a mixture of brave and squaw dress: bare to a slender, strong waist with a squaw's apron from which warrior leggings peek out below. Twin Spirit's ripe and expressive lips and almond eyes are highlighted by long, black hair trimmed with beaver fur. Twin Spirit is an eternal go-between, a half-and-half spirit, not a soft man, not a hard woman, with a voice not of man, not of woman. Sometimes I think of Twin Spirit as a he, sometimes as a she. Twin Spirit responds to the needs at hand and his/her aura tells me which pronoun is manifest.

I am myself a compound, a Mormon wife and a Shoshone sister of the sacred ma ai'pots.

"White Cloud," he greets me.

"They call me Sister Sarah."

"In the forest you are White Cloud. I will not address you as Sister Sarah, for here you are ever my Shoshone twin, White Cloud."

"It is only up here at Temple Hill, away from them, that I can again dream of being White Cloud. Down below I am a Mormon wife."

"Remove those Mormon shoes and walk with bare Shoshone feet on this sacred earth."

"No, I cannot." I reject Twin Spirit's temptation.

I have dreams where I am dressed as a warrior and go out to hunt game. I am on the warpath with other braves ready to kill and scalp. Like Twin Spirit, a part of me is male. The horses recognize my power over them. But had not Chief Sagwitch given me as a wife to the Patriarch so that I, sacrificed in my womanly side, might be meekly assigned to his rooster-like coupling in that sainted bed?

Twin Spirit comes with a full sack of aromatic plants, flowers, roots, and mushrooms. He offers some of the finest to me. I will not tell the others that I have accepted Shoshone gifts. I search for the edible black, yellow, and white morels that Sister Hannah covets. I place them in the safety of my medicine bag. I pick but then reject an amanita, a false brown morel, only good for poisoning the wicked. Twin Spirit adds it to his burgeoning sack.

"Are you sure you don't need some amanitas?" Twin Spirit offers another. "Perhaps there are animals that need be poisoned."

"I will add them to my bag." I do not look up. "I need some spotted cowbane to poison the rats. I must go to the pool on Sweetville Creek."

"I will accompany you there if that not be too close to the Mormon settlement for your comfort?"

"You are a ma ai'pots and must go where you must."

As we approach the rich, deep grass of the largest pool of Sweetville Creek, a gentle splashing of water comes from the pool. The aspen leaves, usually so quick to quiver, lie limp and heavy. The rigid, spear-pointed silver spruces encircle the hush of the pool.

CHAPTER TWO

No slender blade of grass dares move. I stop but Twin Spirit takes me by the hand and leads me closer.

"Who goes there?" I finally ask.

"Evan. Do not approach, Sister Sarah, for I hath shucked all proper clothing. I am without my Mormon garment and am not fit for a woman to behold."

"I have come here with my brother, Twin Spirit. Finish your bathing while I gather poison for the rats."

I stay close enough to spy them through the leaves. Evan and Twin Spirit first stay apart. I have no trouble finding the water hemlock with its distinguishing thrice-divided, purple-spotted leaves and dig deep for its toxic roots. I find abundant toxin for the family's needs.

Twin Spirit advances on to the stone-bedded pool. Brother Evan's white skin reflects brightly in the shallows. "It is good for the body to soak in the clear, sweet, pulsing waters. Nature softens the warrior's hardness," Twin Spirit intones.

I had told Brother Evan about my ma ai'pots brother, but this is their first meeting. I watch them as a Shoshone without shame. Brother Evan notes Twin Spirit's full head of straight, black hair. He takes in Twin Spirit's upper half naked to the waist, and the skirt-like costume and warrior's leggings that cover his lower half. The two gape at each other unashamed. They seem to have no need for introduction. It is as if Brother Evan and Twin Spirit had been introduced to each other previously by the Great Spirit. Brother Evan pulls himself out of the pool, dries himself, and regains his Mormon garments. Twin Spirit waves to me, he must have known I was watching, and then retires into the warm forest.

I, White Cloud, return to the Patriarch's alien homestead with my medicine bag full of its gatherings.

CHAPTER THREE

Eugene Lannon

JULY 8, 1862
SWEETVILLE

"Mine house is a house of order, not of confusion," Patriarch Sweet claimed as Abigail, Abel, and I entered his abode for our first dinner with the patriarchal family. I hoped that this would be the first of many meals with this extended family, the better to study its inner workings from the inside. I was short of funds—as Abigail was quick to remind me—and needed to find in this Mormon family both Herald articles and the makings of a best-selling Western novel.

Before we sat, Mother Evangeline, as the senior wife, did us the honor of showing the house. Downstairs lay a formal front parlor, a large dining room with a much expandable table, a too warm kitchen with a prominent squared rack, and the best room in the house, the Patriarch's private, book-lined study. Upstairs were five bedrooms. Mother Evangeline took great pride in the Gold Room where the "sealed wives slept." She sneered a bit as she showed the smaller Blue Room. She marshaled us into the Patriarch's bedroom, an austere cell without heat and with a lone, single bed. One dormitory for the still-at-home daughters and one for the unmarried, minor sons completed the upstairs.

This house, grand for a Mormon clan, was so different from the modest cabin where Abigail, Abel, and I were uncomfortably bedded down. That had two bedrooms, one in theory for Abigail and me with another at the opposite end of the one-story building for the solitary Abel. Around the central fireplace were three rough chairs with rawhide covers. Abigail had looked askance at their primitiveness. There was a barely functioning kitchen and a small table. Abigail was not known to cook, so with any luck we would be asked to sup with the Sweet family frequently.

Patriarch John Sweet, without a semblance of courtesy, did not greet his eight wives as they came to the table. He was also their Bishop and their Patriarch. He must not show them any individual favor. The family prayer was offered while kneeling around the table, the blessing on the food followed as the twelve of us sat. The Patriarch appeared hungry and thus he was quick. The prayer and the blessing were short without vain repetition. Abigail, Abel, and I did not kneel for the prayer, but we did lower our heads, either as a compliment to the host or out of the confusion of the un-elect.

"Why only seal those wives that have given you sons?" I asked the Patriarch once the food passing had quieted.

"Those sealed are the just and the true who have been blessed with sons as the first and finest of the gifts from the Lord. Our sons carry on Mormonism. They are carried in our arms, while our daughters need be carried on our shoulders."

"But will your unsealed wives be able to join you in heaven?"

"An unsealed woman cannot enter into the same heaven as her husband as she hath no one to introduce her. An unsealed wife will enter a lesser heaven. Only those who are sealed in the new

CHAPTER THREE

and everlasting covenant of marriage, and who thereafter keep the terms and conditions of that covenant, attain the highest of the three heavens within the Celestial Kingdom. Who are my wives? Who are my sons? Life is a constant search for wives and for sons."

"What of your daughters?" I queried.

"They come as they must. But it is for allotted sons that I must search for—they are ultimately the ones that are useful."

"Is this Mormon orthodoxy?" I asked.

"No," the Patriarch answered with finality. "I have read deeply and thought much and have been given my own gift of Prophecy." I doubted whether Brother Brigham was too pleased at this renegade canon.

Sister Prudence changed the subject. She looked at Abigail's New York-bought silk gown. "Mrs. Lannon, how much must your husband have paid in fashion's ample fee?"

"Oh, this old frock predates my marriage." Abigail gave me a dismissing look. "Eugene could hardly afford me anything new that is comparable."

"Here we learn the principles of a life of obedience to noble men. We need not be flattered with current styles," Sister Prudence said.

"You must keep your garments plain," Mother Evangeline added. "Their beauty must be the work of thine own hands."

Abigail blanched at the suggestion she might need to sew her own clothes. Surely our poverty had not come to that low a point. She ignored Mother Evangeline's urging. She first gazed fixedly at our ample companion, Abel Bermann, and then at the lean Patriarch.

Patriarch Sweet responded by opening his Bible near at hand and pointing his reading at Abigail, "O desolate one, what do you mean that you dress in scarlet, that you deck yourself in the ornaments of gold, that you enlarge your eyes with paint? In vain dost you beautify yourself."

He closed the divine Book and continued to teach. "Be humble, be patient; be prayerful. Listen to the counsel given you, and obey it, and you shall be blest." Little did the Patriarch know of Abigail if he expected her to be the humble wife! It was not her way to meekly obey.

The Patriarch mused on, "I am searching for the ninth of my wives, whom I must convert from iniquity, to make her an Eternal Mother, to join me as the Eternal Father of the chosen seed. Exalted parents, husbands, and wives, arranged in relationships from pre-existence, bring forth their allotted spirit children. The saintly continuation of my seed forever forms a holy generation to the Lord. To bring forth sons."

Sister Nona looked pained by this talk of adding another Sister.

If the Patriarch was correct, then what of my barren marriage to Abigail? Was I her chosen Eternal Father? Was our marriage, tenuous at best, a presumptive choice, not the result of divine edict? What threatened its continuance? The well-fed Abel. The lean, manly Patriarch. I had been told by my editor that it was a myth that Mormon men were scions of unlimited lust attempting to lure whatever attractive women came their way into their harem. But then why was the Patriarch aiming his pointed preaching at my wife?

From Abel to the Patriarch, everywhere around me I saw threats.

CHAPTER THREE

"Without true faith, there will be no fruits of your womb," the Patriarch harangued.

I was not sure that Abigail cared that we were childless. For her, was not our barrenness but another aspect of my much-maligned impotency?

Nothing stopped the Patriarch. "As humans are, God used to be. As God is, you can become. God himself was once as we are now and is an exalted man who sits enthroned in the Celestial Heaven. He has set us a plan of salvation. He has set us up for a test of faith and obedience. If you are ready to sit for your trial, then you will have found an everlasting family like God himself. You too will be ever exalted. You too can become an eternal parent like God. You too can lead your sealed wives into the divine presence."

Abigail traded whimsical looks with Abel.

I looked around the table at Patriarch Sweet's wives, pausing to tote up the Blue Room, second class wives, Sisters Sarah, Willa, Nona, and Katherine, and the Gold Room class wives, Sisters Karita, Prudence, Hannah, and Evangeline. What was I to make of this doctrine of segregation based on the survival of sons?

"How can you live in New York City?" The Patriarch turned his attention to me. "Like Babylon, it is the city of the fallen, populated by a poor, narrow-minded, pinch-backed race of men, who chain themselves down to the law of monogamy, ready to live all their days under the domination of one wife. You must flee this Babylon and find in your flight your salvation."

Did Abigail truly dominate me? Probably, but I was not sure that I had the energy to confront more than one wife, to spread too thin my passions and my allegiances.

The Patriarch turned to me with his final words of advice. "The whole message of the restoration of the Saints falls on the truth or falsity of the Book of Mormon. A voice from the dust, it is not a substitute for the Bible, but a companion to it. Just as the Bible is the word of God if translated correctly, the Book of Mormon is his American testament. It will help you, the weak, become the strong. It will teach you how to lean heavily upon God." He stared at me with challenge in his eyes.

Was my weakness that clear to behold? Was my search for something to strengthen me that manifest?

"Yes, Patriarch," I answered haltingly. I must start again and re-read this book.

JULY 9, 1862
AMONG THE SHOSHONE, CACHE VALLEY

Abel Bermann, my ill-chosen fellow traveler, was sketching for another of his genre paintings. It was hard to distinguish in my memory between the event and the painting that Abel was sketching of the event. Abel was an indefatigable searcher for the picturesque. He copied the style of Frederic Church, although he lacked Church's skill for the apt interplay of light and shadow. Instead he searched for dramatic landscape populated with local color that he could safely craft in his 10th Street studio into yet another enormous, marketable painting.

Abel utilized a camera obscura to position the meeting of the Shoshone, the government treaty negotiator, and the Mormons into proper perspective. The Shoshone sure to capitulate, the negotiator, and the triumphant Mormons were all placed center stage. They were dwarfed by the landscape. A Shoshone wilderness, empty, underused, undeveloped, virgin land, was being conquered by God's colonists, the saintly Mormons. This newly-peopled landscape, no longer rude and neglected, was ready to be mastered and transferred into a real estate advertisement for the developable West. Abel would toil next winter secure in his studio, with the Cache Valley landscape, the Mormons in ascendance, and the Shoshone being colonized, each set in place as on a stage. Then he would properly add oil pigment to the outlines of his sketch to manufacture an acceptable memento of the American West. He would name his painting, Treaty with the Shoshone.

Events did not always match their rendering. Chief Sagwitch, Sister Sarah's father, led the Shoshone braves, who were unarmed except for meager tomahawks and iron hatchets. Abel would, of course, tone down the strength of this Shoshone leader, for though Sagwitch was not tall, he was a noble-looking man whose long, still mostly black hair trailed well past his shoulders. An Indian in a genre painting must not be rendered too majestically. He certainly should not dominate the landscape.

Sagwitch spoke Shoshone, as did the Patriarch, but Port Rockwell, Brother Brigham's man, translated for the uninitiated. Sagwitch's name, Tekwahi Sagwitch, meant chief orator. "Where is the land where our children are now to lie down? If we must leave Seuhubeogoi, our Willow River, where can we go? We cannot hide in the ground like a snake."

James Duane Doty—Abel would cast him as the safe, non-Mormon, truly American representative to Utah—was there to negotiate a treaty. "We must move you out of Cache Valley. Your raiding parties must stop harassing the Mormon settlers."

"The Mormons are not our friends," the Chief said. "They want Cache Valley only for themselves."

"You must go north to your reservation, Tekwahi," Patriarch Sweet (Abel sketched his firm, chiseled jaw) answered firmly. "There I shall gather ye and convert ye. I am your shepherd whose flock has been scattered and peeled. And you are the remnant of my outcast flock that I shall return to fullness. Your bowels ache with the sins of your long outcast state. God, in these last days, works through me to recover you, the degraded remnant of Zion's Lamanites, and reunite you with the Saints. Through me you will be freed from your skin of darkness. For you are children of nature, who are destitute of letters, and I have come to bring you the true book. This be the Valley of your decision. You must choose to join the Mormon Church and find with us sustenance." Sagwitch did not look impressed.

The Mormons around the Patriarch began to chant,

For we are going to the land of Laman
To plant the Gospel standard there
To bring them out from degradation
To a people, white and fair.

Twin Spirit, Sagwitch's oddly dressed offspring, who I had met through Sister Sarah, would not make it into Abel's final painting. He/she was too singular to be included. But as Sister Sarah had told me, Twin Spirit was the tonihunt, or leader of the round dance and other spiritual gatherings. It was he who would stand in the center of the Shoshone camp half-circle, face the east, and pray to the sun. It was he who would pray for rain and abundant wildlife. Though he/she was a ma ai'pots, Twin Spirit was the chosen tonihunt. It was clear that Chief Sagwitch and his warriors trusted Twin Spirit.

Twin Spirit spoke understandably in sister-taught English. "We beloved people. What more could Great Spirit offer us. Leave us free of the wreck of the white man. The game of the Valley frightened away by the crack of the Mormon rifles. The pine-nut trees cut down for fuel. The bunch grasses, whose seed we eat, destroyed by Mormon livestock. Let us stay in the Valley of our ancestors. If the Shoshone forced to go to other lands, we grow pale and die."

"We are here to talk with the Chief, not the women of the tribe." Patriarch Sweet dismissed this aberration of a Twin Spirit. "My Brethren are tired of the Shoshone insults. The constant raids on our horses and cattle by your warriors must stop. We came too late to the slaughter field at Bear River and found there over two hundred of your Lamanites dead, your squaws and papooses badly wounded, your wheat supplies destroyed, your wickiups burned, and your ponies stolen. No one was given assistance by Connor's troops. They had left you with nothing. We have fed you and kept you alive through the winter, but still you continue to harass us. Make peace now or we will join the army to wipe you out."

Doty intervened. "I see your children, lying on their bellies on the margins of the streams, cropping the young grass. If you move north to the reservation, I will promise you clothes to clothe their nakedness before the next snow falls and ample food for next winter. If you don't agree to this treaty, you will starve."

Sagwitch replied to Doty, "If your Great White Father so powerful, how can he let the Mormons drive us out of our Valley into the northern mountains?"

Sagwitch paused and turned to address the Patriarch in Shoshone. "I have tried to make peace with you Mormons. I want no blood upon my land to stain the grass. I have given you my daughter, White Cloud, as your wife. But the hearts of the Shoshone are very bad against the Mormons. You have stolen our Valley and called it your own. If anyone does, we own this land that the Great Spirit has given unto us. We have not given it up to you."

The Patriarch answered back quickly, "Tekwahni, the Shoshone did not own this Valley that we have come to give form. To develop this land is the Manifest Destiny of the Mormons. God has willed that the Mormons shall take refuge in this land for this be part of Zion."

Abel glanced up as the Patriarch spoke. Here would be the focal point of his painting. Here was the hero of the narrative his hues would tell.

Tekwahni Sagwitch closed his fist and placed it against his forehead, turning it to and fro to register his anger. He then extended the two first fingers from his mouth. His sign said, "Patriarch, you lie!" He then seized an imaginary object with his right hand from under his left fist and motioned to the Mormons. His sign said, "Mormons, you steal!"

"Will you smoke the calumet of peace?" Patriarch Sweet asked, already knowing the answer.

"Will you sign the treaty and move quietly to a reservation in the north?" Doty asked.

CHAPTER THREE

Sagwitch spoke. "I am tired of talk that comes to nothing. How smooth is your language, spoken with a crooked tongue, that can make right look like wrong, and wrong like right."

Sagwitch waved his hand furiously from right to left, as if motioning the Federals and the Mormons away. "No!"

Sagwitch gestured to Twin Spirit and the other Shoshone. They all mounted their horses and rode away.

Port Rockwell turned to the Patriarch and said, "You never can trust those snake diggers. They are only fit to be given the blue pill, a shot in the head."

Before we left the clearing, Abel turned to me. "Well, Eugene, the Shoshone will come round I am sure. I already have my painting blocked out as a treaty in the making. We can't let a few complications spoil its composition."

Later that day the Shoshone would ride their horses into Sweetville, trample some gardens, steal a few cattle and horses, and take the supply of bread that Sister Willa had kept at hand to placate them. The Patriarch was not bothered. He wrote another note to Brother Brigham, but he did not ask for additional support from Salt Lake City. He could handle them himself. The Sweetville Mormon militia continued to train in the field under the watchful eye of the Patriarch, their Colonel. The Patriarch knew that the God of the Latter Day Saints had given the Mormons a secure home in all of Cache Valley and that He would intervene to make sure they kept it.

CHAPTER FOUR

The Testimony of Sister Karita, Seventh Wife

JULY 10, 1862
SWEETVILLE

I am hungry. I am thirsty. I go to the water bowl. I drink deeply as if there is no tomorrow.

I have been talking much to Lannon, the Eastern writer, about our Sisterdom and the past. I want him to write about me, for my story is the most interesting of the Sisters. I am the most noteworthy of the golden, Celestial wives. Mother Evangeline is too aged. Sister Prudence is but a writer. Sister Hannah just speaks in tongues. I am the ideal Sister, the ideal wife. The Patriarch comes to me willingly, I who satisfy him.

"I am the golden one," I attest to Lannon. "Build a tale around me."

I remember too well the Willie Company and the early morn bugle call. What was this noise calling me to march on the trail to Zion? Could not we just wait and depart at a more sensible hour?

But no, that was not why I stirred myself. Those ordeals were over. I had forced myself awake not out of necessity but out of expectation.

CHAPTER FOUR

I awaken more fully by focusing on the arrival of my admirer, Doctor Peter Jacobson, Sweetville's lone doctor. He comes early this morn to the Patriarch's house to check on Sister Willa and her impending delivery. At least I will have no role in that bloodied affair. Though it will be Sister Hannah's job as midwife to see Sister Willa through the actual birthing, Doctor Peter is not one to abandon one of his charges completely to another's hands. Just like dear Brother Peter.

With timing impeccable, I answer the front door at his first knock. He looks surprised to see me up so early.

"Sister Karita," he blushes.

"Dear Brother Peter." I offer my hand. Peter is mine to play with, an expendable plaything.

"How go Sister Willa and the child yet to be born?" Peter asks after patting my hand.

"She and her child are fine. Their fates are in the hands of our Mormon God," I answer quickly. Sister Willa is nothing in the floods and waterspouts of the Mormon God. Our Mormon God in all of His practical worthiness has more important things on which to cast His care. Sister Willa must not give birth to a son. She is not worthy of Gold Room status.

Doctor Peter looks me over with pleasure. I am an expert in what I look like. I know how to present myself. By form, I am still a fresh and blossoming woman, although I am the sealed mother of two Mormon sons. By height I may be but five feet, but I carry myself with the stateliness of a taller woman. My face is magical. My complexion is still marble struck through with a flush of rose. My hair—it was my hair that had attracted Peter when he followed me cross-country some seven years earlier—is true blond, almost white, with waves that droop low behind. I wear a crimson red ribbon in my hair. I flaunt the ribbon to bring out my eyes, their retiring, reluctant blue-gray. I know what sets my beauty off.

"And how is the Mormon God treating my Danish Karita?" he says, tempting me by withholding the word 'Sister'.

"I have found acceptance of Him and his surrogate, the Patriarch, the father of my sons," I answer with a strict matter-of-factness. Slowly, not fearfully, I move back from the doctor to emphasize the safety and comfort of my surroundings. "He is forever the source of our beneficence." I leave Peter unsure whether the "He" is the Mormon God or the Patriarch. I do not distinguish between the two, for both are so eminently bountiful.

"Were that so, I should join you in trusting Him. I seem to become more each day a Jack Mormon, caught in a ritual that I do not believe but cannot abandon." Peter looks at me without a shred of accusation. He knows why I have chosen the Patriarch over his more pressing, if modest, attentions. I have seen too much to take on an unwanted risk. I have seen death from starvation's want close up—no more eating bran shorts of corn or wheat for me. I take no chances. The Patriarch's position is impregnable—a landowner, a businessman, a Bishop, a Prophet, a seer, hopefully soon a member of the Church leadership, the Twelve. The Patriarch, a man of ample harvests, has the means to support as many wives as he might choose. And I am one of his higher, Celestially-sealed wives, the most fecund of the golden wives, the one he asks for willingly and often.

I was the first of the Patriarch's multiple wives to be sealed openly before the Gentiles' prying eyes. The sealing had been proudly announced in the Salt Lake City Deseret News. Polygamy, hitherto the well-known Mormon secret, had by 1856 come out into the light. The Patriarch displays me with pride.

Mother Evangeline joins us in the front hall of the house.

"Sister Karita, what is that crimson ribbon that you are wearing in your hair? Who are you trying to entice with your vanity of apparel?" Mother Evangeline looks at Peter and me with skepticism. "And don't you be luring the Patriarch with your amorous flirting! He has God's work to do," she says with an edge to her tone. How shriveled is her countenance compared to mine.

Amorous? I remember too well starvation to ever be amorous. Although I am quick to answer the sexual callings of the Patriarch, I look upward and away throughout each act. Afterwards I drink and eat to replenish myself.

Mother Evangeline angrily snatches the ribbon from my head.

I do not design to register any anger. I slowly rearrange my hair, removing any hint of muss. "At least I have living sons and have been sealed for them properly in the Endowment House in Salt Lake City safely away from all Gentile eyes."

I remember the cool water in the blessed fount atop its twelve, white, wooden oxen. The sealing ceremony called forth heaven's blessing with a solemn prayer, a united shout, a Hosanna to God and the Lamb, then an Amen, another Amen, and another Amen. How safe I felt, at last re-baptized and sealed. The Patriarch was then my eternal marriage partner, exalted to become a God. He was clearly a God in the making; he would have no end, everlasting to everlasting. And I had earned the right to sit by His side in the Celestial

Heaven as a Mother of Israel with my two healthy sons.

I taunt Mother Evangeline, "I have not been granted Gold Room status in mere memoriam for a son who did not live to see his manhood. I have living sons."

Rage as hot as ashes crosses Mother Evangeline's face.

"Mother Evangeline, I have come to check on Sister Willa," Peter says to keep anger's fire from relighting. "How is she doing?"

"She is upstairs and doing fine. What would she want with a doctor? Birthing is women's work. Sister Hannah will lead us. Our Sisterdom will have to be enough."

"I just wanted to see that Sister Willa is healthy. To see if she needs anything."

"You men! Thank God the Patriarch is not as sentimental as you, Doctor. Well, if you must. But do not be touchin' her. I will go fetch her." Mother Evangeline leaves us alone.

Doctor Peter looks that insipid Sister Willa over quickly, not one to touch her even lightly without reason. She, of course, is blissfully healthy. Would her not-yet-born child be male or female? Did a Blue Room or a Gold Room future await Sister Willa? God help us, lest the Gold Room become overcrowded with those who are unworthy. Why would God waste time elevating any of my Sisters? They are but pale reflections, mere handmaidens, next to my beauty. I am the best and shall remain the best. Who could question that?

Peter's rationale for visiting our house is now dispatched. Reluctantly he parts without looking back at me again. There cannot be too much temptation in one short day for poor, not quite the Brother, Peter.

Sister Sarah enters with the morning's washing. She hands me my newly cleaned undergarment.

I raise it high, flaunting it before that red renegade.

"I received this at my sealing. It is a sacred cloth that protects me from harm head to foot." I hold it up proudly.

"For me it would be too warm to wear in the height of summer," Sister Sarah observes like a Shoshone.

"I fear only the cold, not the heat. I feel safe only when I am warm."

"If I had to wear such vile garments, I would feel like a deer caught in a snare."

"No Lamanite arrow or bullet can penetrate me when I don it. But then you are one of the dark-skinned ones and do not need such protection."

"I am the Great Spirit's child. I need no other sheath," she counters.

Sister Sarah and I gather the lunchtime food to be brought to those tilling the fields. I cannot stand her presence. Such a Shoshone squaw with such inky blackened hair.

At least the wagon arrives on time. I cannot walk. I will never walk again if I have my choice. I marched all the way to Zion with the Willie Company—and that was enough walking for a lifetime. I perch myself high upon the Patriarch's wagon-top, reveling in the breeze's play upon my tightened bonnet.

NOVEMBER 6, 1856
ON THE TRAIL

The Company led by the honorable, if hapless, Brother James Willie was persistently late. The Scandinavian Mormons, most bankrolled by the Perpetual Emigration Fund, had been late sailing from

England. They were late arriving in New York City. They were late in their journey to Iowa City where the Trail itself started. It was mid-July before the Willie Company was ready to depart. The Elders were divided in their judgment as to the practicality of reaching Utah so late in the season. After all, we still had a 1,200-mile journey left to Zion. Brother Willie led the decision that, God willing, it was not too late. The Elders thought we could in safety journey to the resting place of Israel in this, the latter days. But of course we were too late.

Few of the Scandinavians, and certainly not me, Karita Hanson, or my younger, lesser sister, Elsa, could afford to ride on a wagon. There were only six wagons when the group left Iowa City—six wagons for five hundred people. The Mormon planners had called this new concept, a handcart train, "Zion's Express." There were some one hundred twenty handcarts, each loaded with one hundred pounds. We walked and sometimes we pulled a light handcart, nothing more than a rickshaw. "With speed we will strengthen Zion," the Elders claimed. They had promised the cart would be light enough that even a young girl might draw it. They were wrong. Lying our way to Zion. The handcarts would lessen the time and the expense of emigration. Let them gird their loins and walk through to Zion.

They had promised the handcarts would be swift and sure. They were neither. Fallible carts, even those pointed towards Zion, still lost their wheels. The unseasoned wood of the handcarts had long since shrunk, warped, and cracked in the dry, summer heat. Some of the axles were made of wood. These were prone to grind away in the dust. Metal axles needed greasing and for this the Willie Company had no more bacon left.

CHAPTER FOUR

"At least they have stopped singing that infernal song." I shuddered as I thought about that false, misleading tune.

The chorus clamored,

Some must push and some must pull
As we go marching up the hill,
As merrily on the way we go
Until we reach the Valley, oh!

The Company tried to average twenty miles a day, but even if conditions favored us, we clocked at best fifteen. As our Willie Company traveled deeper to the West, the weather became more severe. Each night became colder. God, I was cold. Would I ever be warm again?

Doctor Peter Jacobson, although a recent convert—my follower, more than Zion's—had been chosen tent captain for the group of twenty that contained both Elsa and me. Peter may have been lax in guaranteeing the daily singing and praying, but he was adept at maintaining peace amongst our twenty. It was Peter's main job to keep the carts in some semblance of order. As our group of four handcarts reached a steep hill, all four of the carts balked; they could not be pulled up it. Peter led some of the stronger, younger men who, with their collective strength, doubled back to bring up two carts at a time a short distance, then back for the other two laggards. Up, back, up—after hours of toil, our whole company gained the summit. Then the carts rolled giddily downhill, out of control in the cold, whipping wind. Then there was another summit with more laggards to be coaxed up. And another. And, of course, it was so cold.

The carts moaned and growled, screeched and squealed. I had only to hear something akin to their noise and I tensed up. It was only with difficulty that I would force myself onward. I would not be left behind in this cold.

"Pull, pull, pull, these Devil's carts," I screamed inwardly.

At last we stopped for the night. A lassitude overtook my sister, Elsa. She knew not where she was or where she was going. She could not help to pull anymore. She lessened. I had not taken over Elsa's pull time. Although I tried to love my lone sister with as much affection as one orphan can offer another, I resented her incapacity. Why was I responsible for a sister, I who craved servants? Who would be responsible for me? Peter tried, but what was he but a smitten camp follower?

Peter had trouble leading the nightly battle to raise the poles and pitch the tent as the snow eddied around us in gusting fits. There were less able-bodied men to assist. Already three of our crew, supposedly the healthiest men, had died. Four days ago, one saintly, strong Mormon had pulled the cart in the morning, given out during the day, and died before morn. Those who remained alive had their strength tempered by the wintry wind. At last the tent was up and there was a warmer place to rest quietly through the enveloping night.

Today Elsa had tried to keep up walking, though she could not do that for long without dizziness overtaking her. She would stop and eat some snow. She ate nothing now, just hard, frozen snow. It was only the doubling back for stragglers that allowed her to keep within sight of the group. Elsa, lesser Elsa, not-my-responsibility

CHAPTER FOUR

Elsa, had lost two toes, the small toe on each foot, to the cold. As a result, her balance was not good. But certainly, no matter how poorly she felt, she did not have enough money to ever buy a ride in a wagon. Nor would she accept the charity of a free ride for the sick. If she could not make it to Zion on her own, then that was God's will, which she must accept. I was tired of her incapacity.

Elsa lay down alone in the tent. Warmer, yes, but Elsa, her enameled lips burning with fever, flashed hot and cold under her inadequate blankets. Elsa may have dreamed of her lost sunbonnet that had fallen into the Platte River as we crossed on a distant, warm July day. Little did Elsa know that she must forge her way to Zion bare-headed.

The Company had not brought much in the way of cattle for food. Each hundred had started with three milk cows and a few head of cattle. "Let us not tempt the thieving Lamanites with too many head," Brother Willie had said. Our paucity of cattle had really been more a matter of money. Most of our Company was at the end of our tether. That was why we all dreamed of the opulence of God's land. Who could afford to lead a head of cattle to Zion? The few cattle that left Iowa were now long gone. There was no milk and no succor of meat from which to rally our strength.

I was never so hungry in my ever-starving life. I could not hear the Prophet's voice anymore. I no longer trusted that I would join the other Saints in Zion.

Peter joined us and built a fire. We lived on Johnnycakes and corndodgers—how I now hate their mealy grittiness—if I had the strength to batter and fry them. Wordlessly, I made this same measly meal. Elsa was long asleep before our fare was ready. "Let her sleep," Peter said with a bitterness that belied his doctor's craft. "Eating will do her little good, for she has no energy left to rally. She is not like you, Karita, a Danish oak with strong roots. She will not make it to the fabled Zion."

I divided Elsa's share of the food with Peter, and mine was the greater quantity. I must be fed first, amply.

I looked numbly toward the tent of my failing sister and then at the soured physician by my side. "You must decide," Peter said haltingly. I gave no answer. Decide? Why must I make a decision when there were not enough choices available? Was it Peter with his childish love built on the beauty of my tresses or nothing at all? Had I journeyed from my land of woe to give myself to a mere struggling doctor? Had I almost made it to Zion for this?

"Peter, who will serve me?" I asked.

"Karita, I will," he answered.

"But what makes you think your service will be at all adequate?"

The five groups of a hundred gathered for their nightly prayer. I spied where Sister Inge hid some dumplings under her false and prosperous wagon. When Sister Inge was invested in the vigil, I left the prayer meeting, found the dumplings, and hid behind the wagon as I devoured them all. I would do anything to survive.

I returned to the still vacant campsite. I heated some snow to make water for my illicit tea. The Word of Wisdom might condemn the drinking of tea, but it remained my only luxury. I had hoarded my pound of tea throughout this cross-country journey and would not deny myself this, the ultimate, sustaining extravagance. My tea was my warmth.

Elsa's life that night went out as smoothly as an oil lamp ceases to burn when its fuel source is gone. She did not awaken to face the fear of death. Her spark went out haplessly in the cold, indifferent night.

I registered no surprise as I fetched Peter. "She is gone. She is now safe in her long home." I did not feign caring.

Early the next day, Peter, with two young men to assist him in their sad, indifferent task, added Elsa to the three others from the Company who would share a common grave. They were buried stiffly wrapped in the frozen clothing and bedding in which each had died. As Peter stood over Elsa's communal grave watchfully, he fired his gun into the air to keep the hovering crows and buzzards away. The smell of the buried, wrapped flesh would bring the wolves to devour Elsa's body. I knew this. But tired and detached, I would not think about it.

Brother Willie led the short ceremony. "Take them, O Lord, and make them ready for Thy kingdom." The internment was accompanied by the plucking of our blind harpist, Brother Thomas. The first deaths had been a shock to our Willie Company, but now it was ordinary to start each day by burying the old, the young, and the infirm. Those, like Elsa, who had given themselves up to death's apathy.

As the last of the harp's arpeggios sounded, the Company heard loud sounds from Zion's way. Ten wagons appeared on the horizon heading eastward towards us. Was this a mirage or had help finally arrived?

"We have come, brave Mormons, to welcome you to Zion. We have foodstuffs aplenty, and wagons for the weary. Turn away the cold and the storms for ye have entered Zion," the Patriarch, John Sweet, bellowed from his lead horse.

Before we continued our journey, I tugged our cart to the edge of the road and gave it a push and watched it roll and crash and burst apart. I would see to it that I rode in glory to Zion. And, that I might never walk or pull again.

All that I brought with me was the clothes on my back and the last of my tin of tea.

As we cleared Little Mountain in our approach to Zion, the Ballo band came up Emigration Canyon to meet the Willie Company. They played a complacent tune, "Home Sweet Home". Unready to accept such tuneful solace, I wanted to stop my ears. Where was Elsa if this was indeed our home?

But I was riding now, secure in the Patriarch's wagon. I looked westward into the Valley with acceptance. So this was what a miracle was. No longer thinking of Elsa's death, I was almost glad as I looked ahead. I turned to the Patriarch, who was mounted next to me. He has already spotted me, I thought, although he has not yet spoken up. But I trust enough in my attractions to place my fate in his far abler hands. I would have this Patriarch to worry for me. His success would guarantee my own. His accomplishments would reflect upon me. He looked at me assertively. He found in me an echo of his assurances.

JULY 12, 1862
SWEETVILLE

The slender, sinewy Eugene and the fleshier Abigail Lannon join our Patriarch's wives for milk and strawberry pie under the sprawling oak out back. Abel Bermann, although included in the invitation, has sent his regrets. Abigail says he is too busy reworking his sketches to accompany the two. She tells of the painter adjusting the spacing on his sketch to more properly accentuate the role of the Patriarch. Certainly that is a fit and proper undertaking.

I watch the Lannons up-close in an attempt to understand them. Abigail Lannon is a female born to use others. She is almost flirtatious with the Patriarch, as flirtatious as a woman can be with my strict husband. I have seen the way she looks at the painter, as if testing a conquest. The writer, Eugene Lannon, I do not understand, though I have talked with him as the Patriarch commanded. Lannon's dark eyes are haunted with gloom and doubt. His confused, expressive face has too much of a woman in it. Why has he come to Zion? Is he merely a reporter looking for a story? What else is he seeking?

"Fetch my tea, Lamanite," I order Sister Sarah before she can sit down. "I have had a hard afternoon seeing to my sons. I'll have a cup of tea with my pie. Then I may lie down in the Gold Room."

Sister Sarah will do as I bid without comment. She will put the water on. She will go to the proper slot in the Mormon square rack for the Mormon tealeaves that only I use. She will measure an appropriate amount into the teapot and add the boiling water and let it brew. "Let the Celestial wife have her cursed tea!" she will think but never say. Sister Sarah will pour a healthy cup and over-sweeten it with an extravagance of honey, just as I like it. She will empty the teapot carefully. She will in mockery humbly join us and serve me, a Golden One, as is my due.

"I thought Mormons do not drink tea," Lannon observes.

"It is only Sister Karita who does," Mother Evangeline explains.

"It is a pre-Mormon sin she has brought from her Danish homeland."

Sister Nona, her pear-shaped face hidden by her dark hair as if she might retire behind its strictures, is charged with the pie. She joylessly cuts the pie into ten equal pieces as Sister Katherine pours the well-creamed milk. The Patriarch, too busy with his Bishop's duties, does not come to table. Without the blessing of the Patriarch's prayer, we do not pause before starting to eat.

I add some additional milk and sip slowly the still hot tea. I revel in the tea's aroma and the honey's sweetness.

"Why did you journey to Utah, Sister Karita?" Lannon asks.

"There was nothing for us in Denmark. My sister, Elsa, and I became Mormons and knew that our safe haven was in Zion."

"And what became of Elsa?"

"I told you. She died on the trail." I begin salivating as I remember Elsa's death.

"Oh yes, I remember. We talked of that the other day," Lannon says.

I feel spittle form on my lower lip. I wipe it free with my napkin but then there is more spittle. My wiping cannot keep pace with the accumulation of spit. I froth at the mouth. I begin trembling.

"Are you alright, Sister Karita?" Mother Evangeline asks. "Perhaps you should go lie down."

"Yes, maybe I... I should." I slur my words. I try to rise but am too weak. My quivering muscles will not obey. I try again to get up, but just then, a violent tremor passes through me. I knock the teacup over, its contents spilling to the ground.

Lannon rises to catch me lest I fall. How could I, who am paramount, ever fall?

CHAPTER FIVE

Eugene Lannon

JULY 12, 1862
SWEETVILLE

I looked long at the milk and at the empty cup of tea but said nothing.

"Fetch the Doctor," Sister Katherine ordered Sister Nona. She obeyed with a glassy eye.

"Find the Patriarch," Sister Katherine ordered Sister Prudence.

Sister Karita was having heaving seizures by the time Doctor Peter got there.

"Karita, what is wrong?" Doctor Peter asked plaintively.

Sister Karita, savaging for a breath that would not come, could not answer. She spoke instead of her missing sister. "I am coming, Elsa, I am coming. You will keep me warm."

The Patriarch arrived and retrieved a small vial of consecrated oil from his key chain. He tried to soothe her by laying his hands on her. As the Patriarch touched her one last time, Sister Karita convulsed and was still.

"Karita!" Doctor Peter reached out to touch her.

The Patriarch swatted the Doctor away. He ignored the Doctor's inappropriate personal grief. "Sister Karita, my birth mate of sons, wait for me in the Celestial Heavens, for it is there that I will join you."

Doctor Peter was not invited to the hasty funeral and internment later that afternoon. It was an affair for only the Patriarch, dressed in Bishop's robes, and his seven remaining wives plus the children. Ever the author, I observed but remained silent. It was only the Patriarch's voice that could be heard before the open grave.

"Funerals are for the comfort of we, the living, who must remain on earth without the blessing of Sister Karita's presence. She does not need our extravagant assurances. She is taken home to that God that gave her life, to live forever in His secure paradise, free from care and sorrow.

"Hers is a grave disrobed of its terrors. It is neither a place of worship, nor a place of devotion to the departed. For why should we need a site for consolation when we know that hers is the blessed state of a well-contented Saint reposing in a sweet valley with those Prophets that have gone before?

"Her reward in the Celestial Heavens is not affected by what we do here. Her place there is set, confirmed by sealing. Some will ask to raise her up now. But no, Sister Karita is waiting in the Celestial Heavens, waiting for our complete chosen family to be assembled there."

Sister Nona looked on stonily.

"Soon, in these final days, the earth shall tremble and reel to and fro as a drunken man. God in his red apparel will open up the graves of the righteous so that they shall come up out of their graves

CHAPTER FIVE

and be a part of the resurrected land of Israel."

Sister Karita's robed body, wrapped only in a quilt, was consigned to its narrow home without a coffin.

The Patriarch remained dry-eyed. He looked at each of the seven wives in turn. He looked approvingly at Sister Karita's two young, terrified sons. He offered them no explanations or assurances. He offered nothing else to anyone.

JULY 13, 1862
SWEETVILLE

"The Patriarch certainly buried Sister Karita quickly. I'd have loved to get access to that teacup or the full teapot. Something was amiss in what she drank," I said to Doctor Peter as I waited for my interview with the Patriarch on his mansion's front porch.

"The Mormons do not suspect foul play. That is just not God's way," Doctor Peter explained bitterly. "If Karita were indeed poisoned, that would not be a Mormon crime. It would smack more of the decadence of the East or of Europe. We have no police in Cache Valley. Who needs them when death or transgression is so obvious and justice so quick? There are no subtle crimes of murder amongst the faithful. If it be murder, we Mormons think it must come from the outside."

"But then who will research her death?"

"How should I know? I'm just a doctor left alone in this Godforsaken place."

"You cared for Sister Karita, didn't you?"

"Yes. I saw her and I was smitten. It was to follow her that I ventured to Zion."

"Then obviously you care about understanding how she died."

"I do," he said with a firmness in his voice. "You are a journalist. Is crime something you understand?"

"I have done some detecting in the past."

"Then start detecting," he said bitterly. "Mormons cannot be detectives. They are too busy being Godly."

"But how do I get access to the family if indeed this be a family crime? How do I detect in this enclosed household?"

"The same way you research any crime, I guess. Learn their stories. Ask questions. Talk some. Listen more."

"How do I start?"

"Start where everything starts in a Mormon clan. Start with the father, the Patriarch. If this indeed be a Mormon murder, he and his story must somehow be at the root. Then try to understand how each of his wives fits into that story."

The Patriarch came out to lead me into his study. He nodded the Doctor away, dismissing his insignificance.

I expected the Patriarch to allude to his wife's death, but he just stared ahead. There was no talk of suspicious circumstances or of poisoned tea. He had no doubt that his wife was safe in the Celestial Heaven awaiting him. Why mourn or doubt or ask questions when Sister Karita's fate was so clear?

"Ask me what you want to know about us Mormons," the Patriarch blurted out. "I shall make time for you. Time to show you the proper path. That is if you seek the proper path."

"Of course I seek the proper path," I replied automatically in my nervousness. I felt a need to placate him, to answer to him as if

CHAPTER FIVE

he was my Father.

"Will there be pressure to remove polygamy to gain acceptance in the Union?" I asked, trying to get him started with an easy question. It helped remove any focus on me and what I sought.

"What Union? We reject this smoldering relic of a Union. If the United States should survive, there will be those in the Church who will argue for capitulation on polygamy if only for a time. But man must have his multiple sealed wives to people the earth at Christ's Second Coming."

"What is the Mormon position on the Civil War?" I asked.

He talked of this Civil War amongst our enemies, this desolating sickness of butchery and violent death, as a sign of the End of Times. It is God's strange work that proceeds the End. It is the appointed Day of Burning when the vineyard will be cleansed of corruption. He told of the short season of preparation that shall usher in Christ's Second Coming. How Christ shall come as a thief, unexpectedly, to reign in glory surrounded by his Saints.

The Patriarch peered yearningly forward. He started to gesticulate and his utterance became more violent.

"I, John Sweet, Patriarch, Father, am attuned to the Lord's presence at my door." The Patriarch looked through me as if I were a subject bowed down before him. I felt his power.

"I, the Lord, have withdrawn my belief in these United States. Be they North or South, they have made their deeds evil. Christ shall be nailed on the cross of neither the North nor the South. The beasts of the earth will winter upon our enemies who have driven the Saints into the wilderness and laughed at our calamities. May each sinful nation of the Antichrist be trodden down equally! Let them break in pieces consumed by blood and fire and vapors of smoke! I decree upon each a proportional destruction."

His speech was awash in pronouns. I felt each I and we. "We, Zion, will be victorious over them. In the future, the jointly defeated North and South will take on a triumphant Church of the Latter Day Saints in the battle of the Great Final Day. I, as God's Prophet, will give my support freely only to those who seek Zion. The Saints shall get all things ready, and when the time comes, we shall let the water on the wheel and start the machine back in motion. We shall stand forth as Saviors. The Earth shall die, be resurrected, and become like a sea of glass."

He paused and looked me over. I felt small before his mightiness. "So come you hence, Mr. Lannon, for now is the time to enlist with the righteous."

I looked hard at the Patriarch, caught in his assurance that I lacked. It was only with difficulty that I remembered my journalist's task.

"I have talked to your eighth wife, Sister Sarah, and been taken by her story. The massacre. Her brother, Twin Spirit. Was it hard for you to decide to wed a Lamanite?" I finally asked.

"Hard? How could doing God's work be hard? We must convert the lost tribes of the Shoshone to make ready for the millennium. Sister Sarah is but the first of the multitude that will be gathered. She is the first to be purified through Zion. If she births me a son, I will be sealed to her forever," the Patriarch said. He was a man pleased with himself. Lust wedded to divine duty.

He had his sights on Chief Sagwitch, who knew that the Shoshone needed support against the Federals and that only the

CHAPTER FIVE

Mormons could offer him ongoing aid. He had only to wait and the Shoshone might come to him. The Lamanites were central to his plan.

"But how will you deal with the Shoshone ways?" I asked.

"Those shall be eradicated. We will have no Twin Spirits about luring Lamanites and Mormons into wicked ways. We must cut out this tumor before it can enlarge and engulf us."

"When I talked to Sister Karita before her death, she told me of her travails in getting to Zion with the Willie Company. Why did you choose her as your seventh wife?" I asked.

"It was not my choice. It was decided in pre-existence. It was then that I discovered each of my sealed wives. My life is but a path to re-find them. Sister Karita was sent to me."

"What of your unsealed wives? Why have you not found them?"

"They are on probation. It remains to be seen whether they be of the sealed and exalted or whether they be mere happenstance."

"Why must a wife bear a son to be fully sealed?"

"I am a Prophet and this is but one of my edicts," he said without pause. "God has told me directly that only the sealed may join me in the Celestial Heaven. A living male child proves a wife worthy of the sealing ceremony. It is only with a living son that I am a true Father who can pass on true Prophecy."

"But what of Sister Prudence? And what of Mother Evangeline? Neither has a living male child."

"Sister Prudence is not sealed to me but to the Prophet Joseph Smith. She is guaranteed to join him in the Celestial Heaven. I am but her helpmate through these final days. Mother Evangeline had a male child who was murdered at Haun's Mill. That was not her fault." The Patriarch paused for emphasis. "She has proven to the Lord, her husband, that she is worthy."

I asked him if most Mormons agreed with him. Was this renegade doctrine? Didn't it keep him from rising in the Mormon hierarchy?

"I will rise, rest assured." The Patriarch had no doubt. "I am already of the quorum of the Seventy, and soon I will be chosen as a member of the Twelve Apostles. The only higher offices are the Three of the First Presidency, and the lone Prophet. When the Prophet dies, the Council of the Twelve Apostles acts as the head of the Church until a new Prophet is chosen." The Patriarch spoke with certainty. "I must sit upon the twelve thrones, judging the twelve tribes of Israel. In my pre-existence I was ordained to be of the Twelve."

"Would I then call you Apostle instead of Patriarch?" I asked, but the Patriarch ignored my inadvertent question. He had higher office in mind.

"I plan on being in place when that mere placeholder, our President without Prophecy, Brother Brigham, shall be called to the firmament! Then let them choose a true Prophet. One worthy to complete another book of Prophecy, Another Book of Mormon. Just as Peter, James, and John ordained the Prophet Joseph to the higher priesthood, such did Prophet Joseph appear to me to magnify my calling. I am the rightful heir, a joint-heir with Christ."

"Are you writing a book of Prophecy?" I asked. Now this would be a proper story for a novel.

He paused. "I talk too soon. You must prove yourself worthy of my confidence. Now you are a writer of wicked journalism and

CHAPTER FIVE

light speeches full of vain gibberish and idle words. You have only the appearance of completeness. You pretend that you know what you are doing. But you don't. Read the noble works like the Book of Mormon and find there a truer and more pressing diction. If you can shed the dour doubts of journalism's hat, if I but learn to trust you, then perhaps you can serve me as a more holy scribe. Read the Book of Mormon and ponder upon it. Start on this great journey towards belief."

The Patriarch rose. I was dismissed for now.

Sister Sarah was on the porch as I left the Patriarch's mansion.

"Where did you get the tea to brew Sister Karita's cup?" I asked.

"From the proper Mormon square."

"Is there still tea in the square?"

"No, I used the last of it. I made a note to tell Sister Willa to order some more tea from Salt Lake City."

"Was it only Sister Karita who drank tea?"

"Of course. She was the only sinner among the Sisters."

"After you brewed Sister Karita's tea, what did you do with the pot?" I asked.

"I emptied it out and cleaned the pot as I have been taught," Sister Sarah said matter-of-factly.

"How much honey did you put in the tea? Was it enough to cover any bitter taste?"

"I added an ample sufficiency just as Sister Karita demanded." Sister Sarah paused. "Is there a reason you are asking all these questions, Mr. Lannon?"

"Call me Eugene, please. It looked to me that Sister Karita drank something she should not have. Her reaction was like someone who had been poisoned."

"Why would anyone poison her?" Sister Sarah asked blankly. "This is a Mormon family, Mr. Lannon—Eugene. We are all taught to love each other as Sisters in Christ. If there be something toxic about, it must have come from the outside." I was not sure if there was any sarcasm in her voice. She spoke the English language of the Mormons like something she had been well-taught.

It was obviously difficult for any in this multifaceted family to accept that one of its Sisterdom had been murdered.

JULY 16, 1862
SWEETVILLE

"Where are you going?" I asked Abigail as she was about to leave.

"Off with Abel. All you do is sit around reading that boring Book. I must do something," she answered.

I had spent the last three days re-reading the Book of Mormon.

"What is Abel doing?"

"Sketching."

"Finding larger-than-life fictions."

"At least he produces something that sells." She fled.

Sales. I had to produce a book about Mormons. Fiction, nonfiction, who cares as long as it sells. I must court success to hold onto Abigail.

I tried again to enter the world of the Mormon Book. I read this Book carefully as part of an author's research. Then, I did not think I was reading something I might believe in. I must make reportage and write a book based on other books. I must fathom Mormonism

CHAPTER FIVE

and capture it in prose. Find a subject for a novel. Find a worthy subject. Every book has its progenitors. I had read a book by Hurlbut that had claimed that the Mormon Bible was based on a Spaulding manuscript. Who knew where this strange Book came from?

Authors, editors, Prophets. Joseph Smith, the Mormon Prophet, had found the Golden Plates and with the aid of seer stones, the Urim and Thummin, translated them. The plates were written by Mormon, a Nephite Prophet, and edited by Moroni, a second Prophet, who appeared to the Prophet Joseph to instruct him on how to translate. I was confused by this flurry of writing, editing, and translating.

I met daily with the Patriarch and asked him the most basic of questions. "Do you truly believe that Joseph Smith found the sacred tablets and translated them with the aid of the seer stones as he has said?"

"Were the Prophet Joseph to be proved a liar who had never found the Book of Mormon as he had reported, still I would believe the Book, and believe that all who do not accept it are of the damned."

"But the writing of the Book was attested to by witnesses, was it not?"

"Yes, there are the three witnesses who swear to the existence of the tablets and the eight additional witnesses who hoisted them with their hands. But ultimately the verity of the Book comes down to faith in its Prophecy." The Patriarch did not look away.

I played the journalist. I asked the questions but pretended not to be invested in the answers. "What of this story I read in Hurlbut that the Book is a rehash of an unpublished Solomon Spaulding romance on Indians as a lost tribe of Israel with a dollop of religion added?"

"That tale is a budget of lies. Hurlbut's hurlings are from a crazed womanizer. Only Joseph Smith, with a little help from scribes, could have been the author of this divine work."

I found the Book of Mormon padded, as if written by a novelist who had a set number of chapters to produce for his allotted monthly serial. It had a studied air of antiquity, a quaint style, and a most peculiar language overpopulated with words of their own flavor. Its automatic phrase "and it came to pass that..." soon rankled. It imitated the Old Testament, particularly the tedium of Leviticus.

I tried to analyze the Book as a novel, looking for the author, in search of each alien, Yankee word, quick with each objection, weighing agreement with disagreement. Was this a travesty, a blasphemous parody, or a divine Book? Was it fantasy or revelation? I became caught in the force of its Prophecy. Like all true Prophecy it told of the past, reflected the present, and projected the future. I, with my innate faith in ongoing plot, found myself captured by its history, its fiction made up of mysterious fragments. What an artistic amalgam, a tour-de-force with its own consistent pace and rhythm! It only lacked a fitting beginning.

"Author? Not translator?" I asked the Patriarch.

"Author; translator. It is pretty much the same for this Book to be true revelation."

The Book was set in America from 600 BC to 421 AD. It was an abridged account of God's dealing with the ancient inhabitants of the American continent. It featured the Nephites, a chosen people

CHAPTER FIVE

prone to periodic, lasting wickedness, and their ultimately victorious enemies, the progenitors of the current day Indians, the Lamanites.

The Book did seem to lack a beginning. It told of the Nephites in America, but it was not clear who these people were or how they had arrived there. I asked the Patriarch about this. "Why does the Book start so abruptly?"

"The first one hundred sixteen pages were given to Martin Harris and his wife, who was not a believer and probably destroyed them. "

"Are they lost forever?"

"They will be replaced before the Final Days."

"And how will they be found?"

"A new Prophet will bring them, and they will be taken as a new, direct revelation from God," he answered with certainty.

"Is that Prophet born?"

"Yes, that Prophet has been chosen," he answered exultantly. "It shall certainly not be Brother Brigham. Everything he reveals is as flat and stale as a shopping list. I am he that God has chosen as his mouthpiece. I go off alone and receive dictation from heaven. I receive revelation upon revelation, knowledge upon knowledge. It pours out to me and from me. My mouth utters words, eternal words. When I am myself again, I lie on my back, looking up to heaven. All is darkness. I have no strength. I pull through. I go home. Then I write."

Was the Book's revelation about to come again? Certainly in this happenstance I could find a work of fiction or nonfiction that I might write.

The existing, I now knew incomplete, Book of Mormon seemed to me a Christ-obsessed book with Prophets who hundreds of years before His birth and crucifixion talk of Christ, the Messiah, with a clear, modern knowledge of his imminent arrival. An early Prophet writes, "We talk of Christ, we rejoice in Christ, we preach in Christ, we prophesy in Christ, and we write according to our prophecies that our children may know to what source they may look for remission of their sins." Ah, to be forgiven in advance by a Man of the future. Jesus Christ finally makes His much foreshadowed appearance and preaches cribbed, cut-up scraps of a redundant fifth Gospel.

I asked the Patriarch about the redundancies between the Bible and the Book.

His impatience showed. "They are similar to the other Gospels for Christ is always consistent." Wouldn't He preach the same in America as He had in the Old World? All the doctrines of the four Gospels must be taught with greater clarity and perfection in this fifth Gospel. For here Christ talked not in parables, but in perfect plainness. It was the keystone of our religion, the Bible corrected and made manifest.

In the Book of Mormon, time thickened into a pure simultaneity of Old, New, Current, and Future times. Although it talked about the past, it was as if its reenactment of an American Exodus was taking place in current time. It was chock-full of predictions of what had already happened. I read the Book with its confusion of doctrines, a plethora of cross-references to the Old, the New, and the American Gospel. It was full of Biblical quotations that were translated into the exact language of the King James Bible.

CHAPTER FIVE

The Patriarch interjected, "Except when the Biblical text had been unworthy or the translator had garbled his sources. Then the Book corrects God's Word."

I was confused. I could not distinguish what I had memorized as a child under my father's hectoring tutelage and what I read now. Where did the Bible stop and this new scripture begin? And what would the world think of a prelude to this newer scripture? I was taken by the notion that God continued to speak through Prophets and their publications. If He had once spoken to man, then why had He tired of this conversation and lapsed into silence? Was not the finality of the Bible, the contemporary dumbness that my father, my much-hated Pastor, had preached to me in my childhood more a heresy than Mormonism? If there was a God, why would he stop speaking?

I asked the Patriarch what my role might be.

"What I need is a scribe, an editor to polish my revelation. I can see and translate but need someone to better craft my imagination. To make it fit. To make it sing. A scribe will be as a son to me."

"I am not much good with Fathers," I confessed.

"It is because you are not useful to them. I offer you utility, scribe. Take up your true pen and serve me. Have faith through me as thy Father, thy Patriarch. I, who know the way, write the Word, and you edit it as my scribe. I teach you the Word. I make you a student worthy of his master. I set you free from your binding tongue, you who must scribe! If you do not answer this call, your life will remain darkened, sunless."

I was tempted by his offer. "Could a revelation be crafted by humans? Someone bound up by his own weaknesses and personal idiosyncrasies? Someone without faith?" I asked tentatively.

"If one person may speak for God, why may not another? God chooses his Prophets and their helpers. You could scribe and in scribing find faith. By fashioning the words of faith, you could find belief."

"What would I get?" I looked tentatively, looking for a way out from the full force of the Patriarch's edict.

"Wisdom, meaning, direction. You have found in the Book the hinge of the door of your salvation. Go through that door. Do not stay on the outside where you will stumble, fall, and be broken. Enter."

CHAPTER SIX

The Testimony of Sister Willa, Sixth Wife

JULY 18, 1862
SWEETVILLE

Twin Spirit barters with his woven blankets. We two negotiate in the Shoshone language that Sister Sarah has been teaching me.

"One bag of wheat flour for each blanket," Twin Spirit says firmly.

"No, one bag, two blankets," I reply.

"But look at the weave. I lead the squaws in weaving. Each blanket is a living thing that we have given birth to. Each is good."

"So is the flour, the best that Brother Evan can mill."

"So trade good for good. I am sure Brother Evan would accept this deal."

"Why are you so sure Brother Evan would take this trade?"

"He told me so."

"Oh, did he! I did not know you talk with him."

"I see him sometimes when I meet with White Cloud."

"I am sure the Patriarch would not approve of your meeting up."

"Yes, I know what that man thinks of me. Ma ai'pots, unclean whore. I take name Twin Spirit after I chose to be a ma ai'pots. I chose what part man and what part woman I am to live as. I am two-fold and one-of-a-kind with the seedlings of the male and the female within me. I am strong like man and lead the women in work. Everyone wants to wear an apron sometimes."

"The Lord's ways are a mystery." I smile at Twin Spirit. "How about three blankets for two bags flour?"

"Accepted. See, the people of the Great Spirit can come to agreement with you of the Mormon God. You Mormons have only to leave us room in Seuhubeogoi. We can share this willowed Valley."

Twin Spirit unloads six blankets from the packhorse. He looks satisfied for dickering with untiring patience and is pleased to get the most food for each of their excellent blankets.

I gesture to a pile of four bags of flour. I had predicted what the terms would be. We both are happy with our trade. Twin Spirit loads up the flour.

Brother Evan enters the shop. "I have brought you a dozen more bags of flour, Sister Willa."

"Good. Bring them in. I have just bartered away the last of our sacks."

I add a dozen sacks to our saintly list.

"I hope you gave Twin Spirit a good price."

"Yes, I always give a proper price."

Twin Spirit remains in the doorway, all eyes, watching Brother Evan stock the flour. Twin Spirit's eyes rake the lean, hardened contours of the miller's arms and shoulders as if putting them on some scale whose weight tested true. No words were spoken, but both nodded in acceptance.

"Will you come this eve to sup with the Patriarch and the

Sisters?" I interrupt them nervously.

"No. I have work to do at the mill and will sup alone on bread and cheese," Brother Evan answers decisively.

Twin Spirit turns to Brother Evan as if continuing some ongoing conversation. "You sing as you grind your flour and your song will be echoed by hundreds more around you. Your hopeful song, weary no more, gain energy. You spread a slender melody and let it live. Come, Brother Evan, sing out."

"You must teach me some Shoshone songs, Twin Spirit."

I dismiss them both with my benediction. "If you but love the Lord, you may sing what you may."

Twin Spirit and Brother Evan leave. I watch them as they go their separate ways.

I, although ripe like a bursting seed, take to dusting the store with a cleanness of spirit. I must never rest, but always labor. I jot down tasks to be done, that which must happen in case I am called away. Quiet, unassuming, faithful, I await my term as I float through each day working for others. For such is the ecstatic vision of the Lord. I need not seek out the Lord. I find Him in each action of my ever-busy life. Life is a feast of fat things given to the just.

Sisterdom is the saintly division of labor. I cannot imagine a Sister who is not wedded to the Sisterdom. I am the tithe-mistress for the Mormons. I run the general store that is the local tithing office and the bank for Sweetville. For me tithing is a liturgy of possessions. I humbly catalog the tithe-work contracted and executed. I keep close tabs on each Sweetville Mormon family's obligations and monitor their fulfillments. I am the grocer for Sweetville. For me each transaction is weighted as if on an ever-present scale. The herdsmen pay in cattle, the farmer hay, the housewife butter and eggs, the miller flour. I grant each a receipt that attests to their good standing that can be traded for their necessary endowments. Mine is the job of protecting the belongings of God's ownership. I focus on each particular, the stellar weave of a blanket, the blessed texture of the flour, the freshness of each egg, or the stark yellow of the butter. Each concrete, near, and divine item attests to a happy, unquestioning Mormon faith of sovereign clearness. For me, God is our partner in the day-to-day rendering of His master plan.

I accept the Patriarch as the head of our family corporation and the manager for our town and stake. As Bishop and Stake President, it is the Patriarch's stated job to set prices for commodities and establish the value of labor. He once observed, "All these properties are mine as a gift from the Lord. When any ordinance or contract is sealed by the Spirit, it is approved with a promise of reward." But I am the day-to-day tithe administrator. I run the actual business of Sweetville. I allocate the tasks of others gently. I actually set the prices for flour: ten dollars per hundred pounds to the Mormons; twenty-five dollars to the Gentiles; one-and-a-half blankets to the Shoshone. To the starving, and the Shoshone are often starving, I am the one who gives away free flour.

The Patriarch is too busy doing God's work as a Prophet. Protected by the safety of our Sisterdom, I accept the Patriarch as a divine leader without shortcomings. When the Patriarch boasts that "every cow he owns produces twice the milk, every field he sows reapeth twice the yield," I do not correct his false, optimistic numbers. But Sweetville, the Patriarch, the Sisterdom, and the business flourish. I plan its expansion. Less than one-third of the men in the town can support multiple wives. But for Patriarch Sweet, we, his many wives, each with her role, are signs of his success as a husband, as a businessman, and as a man. His Sisterdom is God's plan. He has truly magnified us all by his calling.

The probing journalist, Lannon, frequently stops by to watch the tithe office at work. "Is there a conflict between the Patriarch's role as your Bishop and his businesses?" he asks. "Where does the religious duty stop and the business role begin?"

"That is only a question that a Gentile might ask." I laugh. "For us, our religious duties and our business duties are not separate. They are all part of God's master plan. Its individual tasks are always clear."

"And how is it decided what roles each Sister might play?"

"Each Sister has her capabilities. We are assigned in pre-existence to aid the Patriarch. We have learned to worship together, to sorrow together, to birth together, to tend to death together, to work and play and rejoice together, to unselfishly pool all our resources for the good of the family. Don't you share your life equally with your wife?"

"Abigail? No. Certainly not in the way that you Sisters do."

"Jesus empowers us. He is the only person who comes to us without a list of must-dos. He says be a good person and do then whatever you will, whatever you must."

"Is that why I must constantly write?" Lannon asks. "And is it acceptable to partake of my dwindling supply of hashish tablets—can you order me some—in order to write?"

"If it is the Lord's will, then it is acceptable. And no, I don't order hashish tablets. They are the Devil's way."

Lannon guffaws as he had expected both of my answers. "I see in the world a subject to write about. I see in your joint Mormon Sisterdom something noteworthy, a readymade story."

"Then your role is to write about us fairly. May our lives be worthy of your study."

"I am reading the Book of Mormon dutifully, but I find out more in watching you interact. I find teachers everywhere, particularly in the quiet fortitude of you Mormon Sisters."

"We have learned that from reading our scriptures. We act them out daily."

"But how can you accept the Book of Mormon as a revelation from God since its origins are so suspect?"

"Who cares about its origins? Only that it be forever helpful."

Sister Sarah joins us.

"Sister Willa, you must not work so hard. Come lie down away from this heat. I will mind the store," Sister Sarah says.

"Will this one be a boy?" Lannon asks.

Sister Sarah does not give me a chance to answer. "I am sure it will be a girl. It cannot be God's plan to break up the Sisters of the Blue Room."

"Healthy boy, bouncing girl; Gold Room, Blue Room. Whatever God has planned is fine by me." I look straight ahead.

"You must remain in the Blue Room," Sister Sarah bursts out. "If you were to leave, I would miss you as a body must miss its soul. Like Naomi and Ruth, wherever you should go, I should go."

"Perhaps you both will have boys and both journey to the Gold Room," Lannon interjects puckishly.

I nod with doubt-free acknowledgment.

CHAPTER SIX

Sister Sarah reacts with a look of revulsion. "It is enough that I am trapped with the Patriarch. I must retain the support of my Blue Room Sisters to survive."

"How is it for you being the eighth wife with the Patriarch scouting out a ninth?" Lannon asks provocatively.

"It is the little things that he could have done and not the larger things that estrange us from him. He does not have enough love for one woman. What makes him think he can succor eight wives, seven now, or even think of adding a ninth?" Sister Sarah answers.

"The Patriarch is the only source of water in this life, and he is not a broken well," I counter calmly. I pause to take a deep breath. "But I must go now to the birthing chamber for my waters have indeed broken," I say calmly.

"But it is too early for you to birth," Sister Sarah exclaims.

"It may be too early, but that is God's will. Come, Sister Sarah, let me lean on you. You must excuse us, Mr. Lannon, we have work to do. A child to bear."

AUGUST 28, 1852
SALT LAKE CITY, THE TABERNACLE

I, Willa Willburton, soon to be Sister Willa, was one of the hundreds of multiple wives wed that hot August day. The day when the Mormons, hiding their polygamy no more, came clean. We showed the world what we had chosen.

"No longer must we deny the blessings of polyandry," the Patriarch railed in the direction of Port Rockwell. "We are safe in the Great Basin in Salt Lake City, away from those prying American eyes. We will not be persecuted for doing what the Lord has ordained, that which has been divinely sanctioned in the Old Testament. We are here today to proclaim the benefits of multiple wives to the world."

Port Rockwell was there that day too. He was flush with funds from running a saloon for the miners of Sacramento. He was ready, like the Patriarch, to add to his stable of wives. But he was quieter about it. He looked sideways at the Patriarch. Here was a man given to speeches, not action. Talk, vain talk. Port was not one to make proclamations, but to do what was accepted, and Brother Brigham said that "now was the right time." They must own up to what every one had been doing these many years. Port was not a conspicuous wedding man like the Patriarch. "A stable of six? Who has the passion and the funds to take six wives?" Port joked. "I will try to make do with three."

"A good wife is a good thing. The more you have the more good you have." The Patriarch gave his opinion simply.

I did not take much persuading when the Patriarch came courting. "Monogamy leads to whoredom, adultery, and fornication. Just as Jesus was ordained to have a relationship with Mary, Martha, and Mary Magdalene, so is it decided that you must become Sister Willa," he had said. "Come join my family, come join your Sisters. Be wed to us."

I had asked to talk to each of the Patriarch's five existing wives to ask them whether they wanted another Sister.

"I really don't care," Sister Prudence said. "I am only waiting in this life to join the Prophet Joseph in the next."

"Another? Aren't there already too many? Another bedmate,

CHAPTER SIX

another whore?" Sister Nona replied when forced.

"I am forever blessed with sons," Sister Hannah answered. "What have we who are safely sealed to worry about with the addition of another applicant for the Celestial Heaven?"

"Come to us. Welcome to the safety of our Sisterdom," Sister Katherine resounded.

"If he may have five, which is more than one, then why not six on display for all to see?" Mother Evangeline dismissed my question.

I had been in Zion for just six months when I wed. I knew that six wives was not too many, for it was God's plan. Six months after that trek westward. On that trek, I had churned the butter by the rocking of the wagon on the long road. I had raised the bread in transit and baked it in an earthen oven when they stopped for each eve. To be a Mormon was to be fulfilled through the blessing of each divine, daily task.

I had been the natural leader of our trek's group of ten, our organizer, our allocator, of course under the tutelage of a Mormon father. Everyone looked to me for the quiet certitude of detailed direction.

It was now nine months after I had converted in the twinkling of an eye to the Mormon God I had decided upon. Once born to the Mormon God, I stood tall without reflection, ever straight and natural. I did not need to read the Book of Mormon to find faith. For me, it was enough to be around the chosen, to watch and learn from the settlers and now my Sisters, to know that this was God's plan. Clearly, clearer than others, I saw His plan for us all. I knew what must be done.

"But what will I do as another wife?" I had asked the Patriarch after the public ceremony.

"God will find you a job. He always does," the Patriarch answered. And so it was. I did not need to be told again what to do.

JULY 18, 1862
SWEETVILLE

I retire to the seclusion of the Blue Room, there to be attended by my fellow Sisters, Sarah, Nona, and Katherine. We are joined by Mother Evangeline and Sister Hannah. They enter our Blue Room as the Elder Mother and as my midwife. God offers much help to my too early child.

I direct the women to cleanse me. Sister Sarah washes my hips, breasts, abdomen, thighs, and nether areas. Sister Nona, without looking, perfunctorily swabs me. In turn starting with Mother Evangeline, each wife washes each other's feet. Let us all be cleansed before the Lord. Next each Sister anoints me with consecrated oil flavored lightly with cinnamon. I nod to each in turn. Sister Katherine, Sister Nona, and Sister Sarah form a prayer circle as Mother Evangeline and Sister Hannah go about their duty.

"Be ye clean that bear the vessels of the Lord," Sister Katherine intones as she lays her hands upon my head as if stroking some great cross.

"I thank the Lord, the Great Spirit, that I am here to aid you in your time of need," Sister Sarah says. "Let me hear your sweet voice. Let me touch your gentle hand. I wish I could be with you, present in the body as well as the mind and the heart. I wish we both might give birth to another female to join our family."

CHAPTER SIX

Sister Nona, watchful, remains silent.

Of course, the Patriarch leaves the house as my delivery peaks. He, God's Bishop, cannot deal with the bloodiness of birthing. His role in this offering is past.

I breathe easily, humble within the very breath of God, as my contractions rise in intensity. I listen, comforted by my still, small, insistent inner voice. I feel an inflowing of God's help wherein I can relax and throw down any burden of childbirth. Giving birth for me is but another blessed occupation. Another sacred set of events. May this early child be safe.

Sister Hannah speaks up. "I think the voices are telling me that it will be a boy."

Mother Evangeline goes about her duty silently. She does not have to ask me to push harder, for I naturally take on the rhythm of this, my assigned task.

Sister Katherine sprinkles me with fresh spring water. I do not need this sanctification, but I thank Sister Katherine nevertheless. "It is nothing, my divine Sister," Sister Katherine replies. "You are the one who is doing everything."

Sister Nona is not helpful. She looks on askance, feeling each contraction as if it were in her own body. On her face is one thought, "God, let this not happen again to me." Did she not see the hopefulness of another birth?

Sister Sarah looks like she is worrying about her incipient birth. "In sorrow thou shalt bring forth children" she has been instructed. So this is the sorrow that awaits her.

"Do not worry." I reach out my hand to comfort Sister Sarah.

At last my small child comes easily. "A male child," Mother

Evangeline announces. He lets out a feeble cry as Sister Katherine takes him in her arms to wash and anoint him.

He is passed from hand to hand. Sister Nona passes him quickly.

My struggle over, I hear the tonic tone of God's approval. I feel strong. "Fear not, my Sisters. I will not descend into child-bed fever."

"Another living son, another sealing," says Mother Evangeline.

"Another blessing, another opportunity," says Sister Katherine.

"Another fear, another burden," says Sister Nona.

"Another delivery, another child," says Sister Hannah.

"Another Gold Room, another loss," says Sister Sarah, as if voicing some fresh betrayal.

"Fetch the Patriarch for he has another son to meet," I order my Sisters.

The Patriarch enters the unfamiliar Blue Room. He raises his right hand to heaven and commands each of us six wives to do the same. He blesses the oil in his left hand and pours a few droplets onto his newborn son. "The heavens are opening up to you, Sister Willa. You hath given me a tiny son, and should he live, you are now worthy of the Celestial Heaven. I see the transcendent beauty of the gate of the heirs of the kingdom. Come forth with me."

Mother Evangeline, the newborn babe in her arms, looks askance that the Gold Room might be repopulated too soon.

Sister Sarah asks for the child to hold. She wipes his mouth and nose and head with a scented rag.

"I don't like his color," Sister Katherine says. "He is so small. He is almost blue. He is having trouble taking each breath. Get the Doctor, quickly, Sister Nona, go quickly."

Sister Nona leaves too slowly.

CHAPTER SIX

I take the babe in my arms and try to add my breath of life. He continues to gasp. But there is little I can do. My son, the Sisters' son, the Patriarch's son, is not to be. Now is not the time for Celestial Sealing. Now is a time of death.

When Doctor Peter finally arrives, it is too late. My son is now blued in death. "He looks healthy but so small. He came too early," the Doctor says. "First Sister Karita and now this. What is happening to this family? It is as if the Lord could not accept another son for the Patriarch."

"My babe is dead. Our son formed by you in my womb did not live. Thus I cannot join you in Celestial Heaven," I state to the Patriarch as a mere fact without regret. "We have done the best we know how for him, but nothing has done any good. He is gone and I cannot recall him, so I must prepare to meet him in another, happier world. Gather round me, my friends, in the sanctity of our Blue Room. For with you here I need not mourn as those without hope."

I turn my head to the wall. I am ready to fall asleep quietly in the Blue Room. I am ready for whatever tasks God shall assign me.

CHAPTER SEVEN

Eugene Lannon

JULY 20, 1862
SWEETVILLE

I had visited Sister Willa to give my condolences, but she was not at home. She had already returned to her saintly vocation, the tithes of the general store. She was doing God's flawless job. What need did she have of my meager commiseration?

It was so hot that day in Cache Valley that we longed for a thunderstorm. It came before I could leave the mansion with its flashing lightning, roaring thunder, storming wind, and lashing rain. The Patriarch emerged from his study. "Come talk with me, Brother Eugene," he called me as a scribe, a son. I was thrilled. "There is meaning to your attendance. God is in this storm."

As I entered the Patriarch's study, he stopped writing something and closed a document and placed it on top of the book he had been perusing. The book's title I could read, *View of the Hebrews*, by Smith. Was this some other relative of the Prophet?

Death was stalking the would-be Prophet's house, but the Prophet remained focused on his Prophecy. He dismissed my

CHAPTER SEVEN

sympathy for his dead wife and stillborn son with a wave of his hand. He had more pressing things to dwell upon.

"I am a link in a great chain of Prophets," he began. "Moses, Isaiah, Jesus Christ, Joseph Smith, John Sweet. Each continues the other. In these days I alone seek and find revelation from heaven. God has called a new Prophet to restore the gospel, to start the cycle anew."

"But what of the Mormon President, Brother Brigham?" I asked, knowingly goading him.

"He reveals nothing more than the price of cattle. He sees nothing."

"How do you find Prophecy?" I asked.

"I hear and I speak for God. Thus saith the Lord. I am His trumpet," he pronounced. "I not only hear what God has to say, but I am convulsed to the depths of my soul by the spreading darkness of His presence."

He continued to inveigh against Brother Brigham, who he claimed hid his face, afraid to look directly at God. A true Prophet like himself was as close, knowable, personable, engage-able as the God who spoke to Moses and to the Prophet Joseph. God was incarnated within him.

"I feel directly God's love and God's anger." The Patriarch's word thundered forth, filling his study and the rest of his mansion. "Only when God has left can I stand again and regain my body." I shuddered with glee.

I could not separate the meaning of his words from the hysteria of their delivery. What would my hated father, the Reverend, think of John Sweet? He would condemn his presumptive, direct communication with God. He would label such Prophecy the work of the Devil. But even the Reverend would be impressed by his force. I certainly was.

"What became of the Golden Plates?" I asked in all simplicity.

"They were reburied and will be found when they are needed. There are caves with books piled upon books with more records than ten men can carry. I have but to seek them and I will find them. God will move them so they will be near at hand."

"I need you, Brother Lannon," he continued without pause. "I need your editing skills to shape my Prophecy."

"Why do you seek an editor? Why do you court me?" I asked meekly.

"For me words come in hoards, false in their security, hard-edged, without evasion. I need someone to call my faith to account, to prudently tidy up what God has dictated. True Prophecy is a vocation that must have its language tamed and properly cultivated. I am alone now and overwhelmed with God's insight. Protect me from the torrent of His words. Come help me, Brother Eugene, come help me. Help me such that they might understand more of His words."

"But you are already a Prophet, why must Prophecy be improved?"

"So that I can become a perfect man. God is perfect man, a perfect man is God. As man now is, God once was. As God now is, man may be." He spoke now clearly, calmly, as if in a trance. "I shall attain my own Godhood in the Celestial throne of eternal power, helped by my sons, attended by my sealed wives."

He called me as to a son.

The Patriarch spoke his own language with only a sideways

glance to the Prophets who proceeded him. I was taken by the assurance of his delivery. He talked to the inner me in direct dialogue. I heard his language, argued with it, agreed with it, questioned it, made fun of it, rejected it, and finally began accepting it. His words scuttled my prudence. They slaughtered me. In the end I found his affect overwhelming. His voice was full of echoes which filled me.

"And where would we start, since there be a 'we' in this equation?" I asked.

"We will start by replacing the missing pages. We complete one book and then start another."

"And how will the Mormon Church accept this new Prophecy?" I asked.

"Soon I will be of the Twelve, and then of the Three, and then the chosen, true Prophet, for I have access to the source works of continuing Prophecy. And what I will tell will be as true as the Book of Mormon."

"Ah, Another Book of Mormon," I echoed.

"We are all leaving for Salt Lake City for Founder's Day soon. You three shall join us there. When we return to the Valley, you must come back as my anointed scribe."

"I will think hard about your offer and decide." I held out for time to ponder.

"What do you have to think about? God has decided."

Was the Patriarch the voice of God, or was he the victim of his own inner compulsion? I must keep close to him to find out. Here clearly was the source material for my Mormon book. I could feign adherence and penetrate the inner life of this religion. By offering my services, I could go inside to solve the riddle of the Patriarch's prophetic calling. How did he forge his capacity? Did I not envy the assurance of his Prophecy? Was his gift real or illicit? If it be real, then was not this the answer to my own inner questions? If it be fake, was not this fakery the stuff of potent literature?

JULY 22, 1862
SALT LAKE CITY

The Patriarch, the Sisterdom, Abel, Abigail, and I journeyed back to Salt Lake City, this beautiful city of quiet, wide, safe streets, reared in an instant upon a desert site, shut in by the secluding tops of mountains.

The Patriarch and the Sisterdom went to their city house. The Salt Lake House where Abigail, Abel, and I had alighted was clean, the rooms commodious if noisy, our breakfasts promised to be hearty. Abigail and I shared our room nervously, still in name husband and wife, but with an estrangement that became clearer each day. Abel, her adulterous alternative, was situated too conveniently at the next door down the hall. He seemed to be awaiting some clear sign from Abigail. If I wanted my wife, I had to fight for her. Did I care enough to fight?

Port joined Abel and me before dinner for a dollop of home-brewed valley tan. Brother Brigham, ever a businessman, owned the liquor concession at the hotel. His son-in-law, Brother Feramorz, who ran the saloon, served us promptly. Port was obviously not the most strict observant of Mormon doctrine. For him liquor was "no treacherous mocker" to be avoided at the peril of his soul. I was drinking this brew trying to break the fetters of my unsatisfied hashish habit. So far I had resisted the urge to replenish my supply. Even Mormon pharmacies like Mr. Godbe's Apothecary that I eyed nearby had a too tempting supply of hashish pills.

Port was closely monitoring my Mormon studies and in search of any smidgen of information on the Patriarch. I told Port about the Patriarch's solicitation of me as a scribe. "What does Brother Sweet want a scribe for?" he asked.

"For his Prophecies," I answered.

"What Prophecies?" Port asked.

"Who can be a proper Mormon without Prophecies?" Abel asked sarcastically.

"For his book," I continued.

"What book!" Port exclaimed.

"Another book," I stammered.

"Mormons don't need another book. We have enough."

Abigail, Abel, Port, and I walked in silence the short distance from the hotel to the Patriarch's home. We passed the Temple block square, some ten acres positioned at the cardinal points. Its square stood clear of all other buildings. The incomplete, but somehow triumphant Temple already was surrounded by flourishing locust trees and a red sandstone foundation wall.

We sighted many a Mormon family with a comprehensive ampleness similar to the Sweets. There was a fascination in surreptitiously staring at every creature we took to be a prosperous Mormon. I watched longingly as families gathered onto them their sons.

The Patriarch's home was on First South and West Temple, down one dusty ten-acre block from the central Temple construction site. The Patriarch's bungalow house was two-stories high, built of gray stone adobe with a flat roof and a low, shady veranda out back.

The surrounding gardens, watered by a pebbly stream, a man-made, life-giving asequia, were full of flowers and vegetables and the promise of fruit. I spied Sister Nona, the gardener of the Sweet family, not quite smiling as she tended the small plot of sweet earth brought down from the mountains, watered by this crystal-clear stream. I did not approach her. I had learned full well to honor the permanent shadow of her silence. The flowers she cultivated were those of the East—the red French bean, the rose, the geranium, the winter cherry, the nasturtiums, and the tansy. In the evening air, there was a sweet smell of strawberries, those that remained a holdout to the July heat.

The four of us, Port, Abigail, Abel, and I, were invited to dinner served on a large table on the veranda out back. Abigail flaunted her liberated status by wearing a bloomer dress. Her dress clashed with the sober gingham of the now reduced seven wives. The wives took their seats with the four Blue Room wives on the left of the Patriarch, and the remaining three Gold Room wives on his right side. The Patriarch smiled knowingly at Abigail as she sat. He seemed to take her bloomer outfit as a shared joke served up for his benefit.

The Patriarch had other guests at the table. I soon discerned the purpose of this gathering. He was politicking to be part of the Twelve. I was introduced to a slew of Apostles, but Brother Brigham, the key elector I trust, was not amongst them. The Patriarch was due to meet with Brother Brigham the next morn. How I would like to attend that conversation to see upfront the interaction of the two!

CHAPTER SEVEN

The Patriarch's after-dinner sermon was a veritable snow squall of scripture and bombast. "I, who must be of the Twelve, make ready to be the highest Prophet."

He talked of readying a temple for when Christ "shall come to take residence." He spoke as if Christ would arrive tomorrow or the next day at the latest, and that he, Patriarch Sweet, who was the only one to truly know Him, would be His host. Was Christ coming to the incomplete Temple or to the Patriarch's private dwelling? I would not call his sermon fatherly, although its belligerence reminded me of my father, the Reverend.

The Patriarch turned to Brother Caleb, one of the Twelve Apostles, and said, "All that might vote against me are weeping willows." Port looked on in anger. Who was the cowering tree that was against the Patriarch's elevation? How could I get myself invited to tomorrow's confrontation with Brother Brigham?

Patriarch Sweet continued to practice his way of flirtation upon Abigail. "Eat not my bread, harlot, with thy hands defiled." She smirked back.

"There is an opening in the Gold Room," he continued. "I have need of a replacement wife as Sister Karita has been taken from me to the Celestial Heaven."

Abigail kept looking about at the abundant fruits of the Patriarch's labor. "And what would you be looking for in a wife?" she sallied.

"I look for the mother of my sons, worthy to be sealed to me for eternity."

"I would have to be sealed first. Seal first, bed next." Abigail tossed her head back.

"We shall see. We shall see." I seared internally with anger.

The Patriarch glowed like a prize bull.

On our way back to the hotel, I had had enough of Abigail and her inconstancy.

"Must you throw yourself at the Patriarch!" I did not care if Abel heard us argue.

"At least he is a man with a comfortable home. He is not staying in a hotel with a tawdry sitting room and bedroom partitions so thin I can hear Abel snoring."

"Fine. Perhaps you should join the Sisterdom. I'm sure you'd be willing to birth an ample number of sons for better quarters," I spat out sarcastically.

"Don't think that is my only option, Eugene. It is clear you can't provide for me."

Abigail did not hesitate when we reached the top of the stairs. Rather than bidding Abel good night, Abigail, as if privy to some signal, paused. Abel opened the door of his room. She entered, taunting me with a dismissive look.

I could not sleep for the sound of them rustling next door. The sounds blended with the buzzing of swarms of emigration flies. I agonized at each sound.

I got up. I needed hashish and I needed a story to write. Blessedly Godbe's Apothecary was still open. I bought an ample dosage of hashish. I swallowed three pills on the street and pocketed the remaining pills.

Still astir, expecting, awaiting, but not feeling the calming effects of my drug, I had to get up. Venture out. I walked back past the looming Temple site to the Patriarch's house in search of a voca-

CHAPTER SEVEN

tion. The Patriarch was still up for the night surrounded by books and papers.

"I shall be your scribe," I said without pause. I believed.

"First you must be cleansed. Kneel down, my son."

I, who had been fatherless, had a father. A demanding father, but a father nevertheless. I knelt.

"No longer seek the calm in vileness."

It was as if the hashish was no more.

"Purge yourself of your impurities."

I was purged.

"Arise, my son, as Brother Eugene."

I rose.

"God makes use of each of us as befits our skills."

"I have one request." I expressed my will.

"What, Brother Eugene?"

"That I attend your meeting tomorrow with Brother Brigham. If I am to be your scribe, I need to know what is happening."

"Come along. I will teach our anointed President how to treat a true Prophet. One that arrives with his chosen scribe."

JULY 23, 1862
SALT LAKE CITY

The titular Prophet received us in his Lion House private office. It was a plain, neat room, with the usual conveniences, a large writing desk, a money safe, table, sofas, and chairs, all made by the able mechanics of the settlement. There was a look of order, which suited the character of the man for whom a door badly hinged, or a curtain hung awry, put his eye out. It was typical of his mode of acting: slow, deliberate, and conclusive.

Brother Brigham met us without greeting. He had questions. "What is this I hear of you writing a book, Brother Sweet? Is this why you have brought Mr. Lannon? Is he to be your editor?"

"Yes, I am a true Prophet. I have tales to tell. My Prophecy comes straight from the Lord. I come to declare to Zion its sins. Brother Lannon will polish my prose." The Patriarch waved his hand at me with dismissal.

Brother Brigham had a gentle, wry look in his eyes. "Your vain Prophecy needs more than fine-tuning. Prophccy is a gift from God. It cannot be manufactured as if it were a fitted cabinet. I sneer at your soaring fancy, for it comes not from God, but from your pride. You will manufacture a lie from the deceit of your own heart. Anything you write will be false."

"You are the one who flatters himself by taking the title of Prophet," the Patriarch countered. "You see nothing. You write nothing. A true Prophet can criticize a mere President, one who flatters his people with schedules and plans but does not truly lead. A true Prophet is not sent to decide mere meager questions. He is sent to divine God's message. Like a dumb lead dog who has confused the path, you mislead us."

"I have brought the Saints to Zion. And I will protect them here. That is God's charge. But for God's charge I would have remained a common carpenter in a country village."

"I have not come to discuss your leadership. Brother Brigham, it is time that I be named one of the Twelve Apostles. I am ready."

"Brother Sweet, there are many reasons why you cannot

CHAPTER SEVEN

become a member of the Twelve. The role of the Twelve is not to write new Prophecy. Would you stop writing to gain selection?"

"No, I must prophesy," the Patriarch answered firmly.

"Do you not believe in continuing revelation?" I asked Brother Brigham.

"I believe that the Book of Mormon is but a fraction of the full account," he calmly replied. "There is more to be found and more to be published. the Book of Mormon, great and valuable as it is, is only a part of the great library of revealed truth. There will be other hills, another Cumorah, where another will find a room containing wagonloads of plates. The seer stones shall reappear and the translation shall restart."

"When would another translator be chosen? Would he complete the Book of Mormon or pen another scripture?" I addressed the question to Brother Brigham but looked to the Patriarch to see if he had an answer. The Patriarch demurred.

"Who am I to answer?" Brother Brigham smiled and shot his answer at the Patriarch. "I am but a furniture maker: chairs, tables, blanket chests, chests of drawers, spinning wheels, and bedsteads. I am but God's furniture maker helping to perfect Zion. Frankly I don't know where Prophecy will come from."

"Then why do you deny Brother Sweet his gift of Prophecy? Cannot he have found something new?" I continued asking questions.

"Some are true Prophets. Some are vain Prophets." He seemed clear on which category included the Patriarch.

"What else do you have against me, esteemed President?" the Patriarch asked angrily.

"You spread false dogma that only wives who supply sons can attain the Celestial Heaven. A true father must bless and seal all his wives so that he may stand as a true Patriarch to his posterity," Brother Brigham answered calmly. "There are probably but few men in the world who care less about the private society of women than I do. But I pay each of my wives proper homage and guarantee them a place beside me in the Celestial Heaven. I at least protect all my wives!" he accused.

"I give each of my wives proper attention," the Patriarch countered. "I believe that only sealing wives who supply sons is a necessary belief to convince the Saints that multiple wives are needed for adequate company in Celestial Heaven."

I looked at Brother Brigham. "Your rival church, the Reorganized Church of Jesus of Latter Day Saints, led by the Prophet Joseph Smith's son, claims that it was you, not the Prophet, who authored the belief in multiple Celestial marriages."

"That is not true. The Prophet recorded this heavenly edict. Any man who attains a certain priesthood may have as many wives as he pleases. We just had to keep it unannounced until we attained the mountain-walled safety of Deseret," Brother Brigham commented.

"Then why can't I choose which wives I seal and which I do not?" the Patriarch shot back with accusation in his voice.

"That is Prophecy again and the Lord revealeth His secrets only to His true servants, the Prophets. There are some whose spirit is not contrite, whose language is not meek," Brother Brigham repeated his first charge.

"I am a true revealing Prophet who dost receive new doctrine from the Lord," the Patriarch countered. "My new revelations

CHAPTER SEVEN

are not meek. They dwarf into comparative insignificance all the knowledge previously revealed. But where the Gospel is there will be opposition and persecution, for Lucifer will not stand idly by while the Word of God is revealed. How can I not be selected to be of the Twelve just because you, Brother Brigham, are a taciturn Prophet who receives nothing in the way of divine revelation?"

The President paused as his ice-blue eyes hardened. He then aimed his last accusation at the Patriarch. "Proper church leaders are revealed to us that are appointed. If you could not be a true witness to the most blessed of revelation, can you truly become an Apostle? You had your chance to give witness to the divine translation but you balked. You would not be the Twelfth witness so how can you be worthy of the Twelve."

I did not understand this last charge. What had the Patriarch failed to do, when, and why?

The Patriarch leapt from his chair. "Yes, I will be an Apostle. And you had better support my elevation lest I have stories to tell about Prophet Joseph's revelation. I shall become an Apostle, or I be a lone witness who might reject the testimony of what the other eleven claim to have seen. Who are you to dare to blackball me!?" This was his parting shot.

When had there been the lack of a proper Twelfth? What did the Patriarch know and threaten?

CHAPTER EIGHT

The Testimony of Sister Prudence, Fifth Wife

JULY 24, 1862
SALT LAKE CITY, THE TABERNACLE

I, Sister Prudence, must write. Words are presents offered to me by our Lord, the Mormon God. I carry my notebook with me to record, to write down each voice as a receptacle of the Lord. Poems start as lines. Stories as words like the wisp of the wind. I, who do not warrant a desk, carry my desk, my notebooks, with me. I write proudly as the herald of the Prophets. It is the calling for which the Lord has prepared me.

Tonight at the Founder's Day festivities I will hear my illustrious verses intoned in all their glory. Ah, the Tabernacle, where the Saints meet often to feast upon the Word.

I join the other women on the north, right side of the center aisle. As I enter the bench, I bow down in proper homage to the first wife of the Gold Room, Mother Evangeline. She has ordered me to cease to find such fault with the other Sisters. After all, she says, you are but the fifth wife.

I try to ignore the others who are so insubstantial to my fate.

CHAPTER EIGHT

I value only those of the Mormon Sisterdom who are convinced of the absolute authority of the Patriarch as my keeper until I rejoin the Prophet. I cannot imagine a proper Sister who does not work in the service of the Patriarch's words. I acknowledge Sister Hannah almost as an equal, though she is a mother too proud of her grown sons. She speaks her tongues regardless of meaning.

In passing I allow myself a fraction of a frown at that wretched Shoshone, Sister Sarah, clustered with the Sisters of the Blue Room. Unwholesome Lamanite. I do not stop to lecture her that she must choose between her love of the Shoshone and her love of God. She cannot have both. Let the Lord show her the disgust of her native ways. Let her become neat and tasteful in dress. Let her stop gathering noxious, native weeds. Let her attain whiteness in the fullness of time. If the Lord grant it, let her birth a son, be sealed, even if it repopulate the Gold Room.

I nod to Sister Willa, purposeful, showing no grief. She is always so busy with her business, all numbers without words. I ignore Sister Nona, a woman lost in her speechlessness. I attempt a smile at Sister Katherine, the singer who does not know the true meaning of the lyrics that she doth sing.

No Sisters understand my wonderful Mormon poetry. I write for the menfolk. I wait my time. I sit quietly, immobile with the respectability of my status.

Brother Brigham makes his triumphant entry amid the roaring chorus of cannon, escorted by a company of cavalry. Twenty-four young men, twice twelve, brandish swords. Twenty-four young ladies dressed in white add a chorus accompanied by the ever-stirring Nauvoo Band. Brother Brigham rides in a large carriage accompanied by twelve of his wives, spirituals like me, I think, not carnals like that hussy, Sister Amelia, who rides so garishly like a queen in a separate carriage. Precisely at four the order is called. Let the speeches, the songs, and the poems begin.

The Patriarch sits with the men on the south, left side. Even though he sits next to his eldest son, Brother Evan, I know the Patriarch sits alone, without disciples, solitary in his direct communication with God. I wonder why the Patriarch courts that vile journalist, Lannon, sitting too close, so near to the Patriarch. Why is that accursed, sinning New Yorker here in a holy place? What does a Prophet need an editor for? Is not God's direct word enough? And why does he not utilize my skills as his scribe? Am I not the herald of Prophets? A woman as scribe would not pass muster was his answer.

Why is the Patriarch wasting the gifts that God has given to dabble with those beneath his care? Why does he not let his own genius soar to heaven and bask in beams of glory there? The words of the Patriarch are as a crackling fire to me. I obey him not as a mere man but as another Prophet of Christ. The mantle of the Prophet Joseph is descended upon him.

I am spared the inconvenience of carnal ways with the Patriarch, as I was with the Prophet Joseph. I believe in the polygamy that the first Prophet re-discovered. It is the polygamy of the spirit. Surely our Lord will not go back on a principle spoken to the Prophet, one that hath caused so much sacrifice, heartache, and trial. If He would, there would be nothing left of the Gospel. I and my fellow wives and their children would be cast adrift, I would sink down into my bed. The earth would open up and take us Sisters down into an impenetrable darkness. To renounce now would be a lie, a trick of the devil.

The mournful but quickening music continues.

Sister Katherine rises to sing a pleasing song accompanied by an organ and a quartet of debonair violins. Her well-cultivated mezzo-soprano soars to the rafters. She shows off her voice as if something saintly. She completes her air with a flourish and feigns sitting down humbly. I know in her heart that she is prideful. Thankfully some of us have more divine tasks to play.

A mighty chorus responds, "Rejoice! Rejoice! The wilderness shall bloom!"

The Nauvoo bell tolls.

Another chorus rises. They sing out the glories of my verse.

> *Altho' in woods and tents we dwell*
> *Shout, shout O Camp of Israel!*
> *No Christian mobs on earth can bind*
> *Our thoughts, or steal our peace of mind.*

I await my time to speak. I, the dutiful, unrelenting poetess of the Mormon way, safe in my memories of the Prophet Joseph, secure in my support of the Prophet Patriarch, unafraid of the mazy fields of erring, jarring reason, know my charge: that of pondering and recording the fate of Zion. That is my calling, not the bearing of its children. I am bound, sealed forever, to the Prophet Joseph Smith for eternity and to the Patriarch John Sweet for this too long present. I find safety in the boldness of the Latter Days. I have not wed either the Prophet or the Patriarch for the here and now. I wed them for what comes after. I relish my future home with the just of all ages. Let it come soon.

Captain William Pitt's Brass Band, a group of British converts, supplies the seductive strains of cheerful music. I see that vile Lannon's attention has wavered from the relentlessness of choruses and speakers.

The Men of the Twelve, minus one, led by the Three Men of the Presidency, form three groups to dance a French Four together. The Patriarch looks longingly at his rightful, fated place. The would-be Brother Eugene smiles.

As the music stops, I bound up like a cork and begin my rhymes. I glance at Lannon who listens, amused by my efforts. Thank God the Patriarch has not asked him to edit my sanctified verse. I am particularly pleased with the pristine polish of my ending.

Other Prophets find their way
For Prophecy must have its day.
Zion is imminent, e'er to be found,
Its voice clear, its message sound.

I sit down and wait for the Patriarch's turn to speak. At last he ascends the lectern. I know what other truths he will proclaim.

"I bring you word of a new revelation," he begins. Brother Brigham looks angrily at Brother Port.

"Soon the missing pages will be re-discovered. I promise you the riddles of the Word. Another Book. There will be Another Book of Mormon, a predecessor to the divine Prophet's words." Would-be Brother Eugene listens closely. He is always asking questions about the Sisterdom. The Patriarch gives answers.

CHAPTER EIGHT

"The first portion of the Golden Plates is at hand. Word will come soon for there are still true Prophets amongst us. Wait and you shall hear more." He sits down to the consternation of the brethren.

I glow inwardly, validated as the helpmate of Prophets.

JUNE 28, 1844
NAUVOO, ILLINOIS

I recorded the grief. If I did not get it down, it would be lost. My other Sisters were incapable of speech. I chose carefully the words, for this was a Mormon document. I was the writer for Prophets, the one to explicate the flame. Had not He, the true Prophet, wanted me for my way with words? *Sister Prudence, come be my herald,* the divine one had ordered.

I waited with the others for the two boxes to arrive. The caskets were covered by Indian horse blankets and prairie grass containing the bullet strewn Prophet's body and those of the other martyrs. I was a lesser wife of Joseph Smith, not in the front with the first wife, Mother Emma. I was kept to the back row of wives. I waited outside the Mansion House where the extended Smith family resided. It was no mansion, modest, more a large house, five windows wide, of two stories. The house was in the center of this most beautiful city, Nauvoo, built upon an unwanted, wet swamp.

Mother Emma cried out, "Oh Joseph, Joseph, they have killed you at last." She removed the Prophet's watch, struck by the fourth bullet, stuck on the time of his martyrdom.

I remained quiet amongst the lesser wives, waiting and pondering. What a noisy boast hath this age of darkness where the savage wildness of the mobs seeketh innocent blood!

I would not have chosen plural marriage myself, but the Prophet selected me as a spiritual wife to spread his word. I embraced his death, a martyr shot in a guardroom. I called out in words my fate. I would not be judged solely by my actions, but would remain an agent of the true Prophet. He would stand as my surrogate before the Lord. I would be judged by a higher standard, that of my sealed husband, the true Prophet Joseph Smith.

I reflected that I was living in the Dispensation of the Fullness of Times. Was not this murder, this savage wildness of a mob seeking blood, the sign that we had entered the Latter Days? For all who bid to win the high, Celestial Prize must seal their covenant by sacrifice.

I had never known what joy was until I became a Mormon wife, helpmate to the Prophet. I was wedded to the Prophet for only two years. Reluctantly, Mother Emma had deemed me a fit wife. The Prophet valued those who might publicize. But I had only to look at Mother Emma's pinched nose to think that I was picked because I was no carnal threat, no threat at all. The Prophet told his first wife that the relationship with me was spiritual, not earthly. I knew that with me that was true; but I could hardly vouch for those other, more comely wives. Mother Emma got a new carriage, and I found in the Prophet an exalted subject for my writing.

But that joy was now a thing of the past. I understood that he was forever walled off into an epic past by a steep boundary. He was now the unapproachable martyr, the tragic hero. My husband, this humble, innocent, and noble child, was no more. Never, since the Son of God was slain, had blood so noble flowed forth from human vein.

CHAPTER EIGHT

Brother Port, freed from a Missouri prison in time, was there to lend a hand, to bear the coffin to its final resting place. Brother Port, he who had kicked in the door of the apostate press, he who had played so much a part in these troubles, he who had tried to lead the Prophet to the safety of the Rocky Mountains, he who had warned the Prophet that to return to Nauvoo was to court certain butchery, he who had failed as the vigilant bodyguard. His thick beard, black as licorice, uncut at the Prophet's command, could not hide his face from my accusing glance. Port turned to the Prophet's son, "Oh Joseph, Joseph! They have killed the only friend I have ever had!"

Of course, Brother Brigham, ever at hand, that slippery rock, was there as pallbearer. "Why was he persecuted?" Brother Brigham asked. "Because he revealed to all mankind a religion so plain and easily understood, consistent with the Bible, and so true. It is now as it was in the days of the Savior."

I remembered the Prophet's words, "I am the first and the last, I am He who liveth, I am He who was slain, I am your advocate with the Father."

I looked upon the noble, lifeless form of my husband, butchered by the Gentile mob. I knew I had in my saintly husband the clear path to salvation. I clipped a strand of hair from his bloodied head. I pledged to remain silent and wait my time. But how could a writer of prose and poetry ever keep truly silent?

Each man was given a secret name that he was to be known in the kingdom of heaven. The Prophet Joseph had given his to me.

The casket was carried into the house. Most of the Sisters followed it within. I remained, jotting down notes. I was surprised when Brother John Sweet, too insignificant to bear the casket, approached me.

"Sister Prudence," he began.

"Brother Sweet."

"They have decided that you are to come to me." He moved closer to me.

"Come to you? What do you mean?"

"Join my Sisterdom. Each of the Prophet's wives is allotted for their protection." He raised his hand as if to comfort me, who could not abide with comforting.

"But why you? You, who are no one in particular." Certainly they would assign me, the Prophet's herald, to someone more important.

"You were the last to be allocated. No one spoke up for you until I did."

"No one wanted me. Why?"

"I do not know. Ask them. Ask the other Elders." I was not gussied up enough for them. And I was not compliant.

"Why did you speak up? Who are you to speak up?" I stood rock solid in my pride.

"I am a Bishop. I will soon be of the Seventy. I am worthy of you."

"Worthy of the Prophet's herald?"

"I will become more worthy of you. I too am a Prophet. God has started to speak to me."

"What would God have to say to you, Brother Sweet?" I asked disdainfully.

"God finds his Prophets at His leisure."

"And what am I to be to you, Prophet?" I asked boldly. "Certainly

CHAPTER EIGHT

not a receptacle to your passions."

"No, not that. You will be my spiritual wife."

"Even the true Prophet did not ask that."

"Nor will I. I need your wisdom, your words." He stepped back.

"And the Prophet's pedigree?" I confronted him.

"Yes," he admitted. "I seek a Sister worthy of Prophets."

"If there is one thing I can do, it is to recognize true Prophets and help them."

"You will find in my Prophecy truth," he said quietly.

"So this is my allocation. To wait out the rest of this life in your care before joining the Prophet Joseph."

"For your protection." He feigned softness.

"And when will this binding take place?"

"After a period of mourning. After we Mormons have decided what to do, where to go."

"A reprieve to grieve. Time to record."

"You will be proud to join me. I will maintain your elevation. You will be content in the Sisterdom of my family."

"A writer is never content when they are not writing."

"You will be my helpmate. You can help craft my Prophecy," he promised.

I turned to Mother Emma, who was listening to some of my conversation knowingly with Brother Sweet. She dismissed me with nary a parting glance.

I was sealed to the Prophet Joseph with his God-like intuition for eternity. He was my hearth, the crown of my life. Let my remaining mortal time with Brother John be blessed. I must work to make him worthy of my widowhood.

JULY 25, 1862
SALT LAKE CITY TABERNACLE BAPTISMAL

That soon-to-be Brother Eugene, the vain scribbler, awaits his turn. He is ushered into the pool by the swarthy hands of Brother Evan, the Patriarch's son. The ceremony is brief, as there is not too much time allowed for dithering in this pool, the sacred Baptismal Fount, deep within the Tabernacle. Baptism in a bathtub is not proper. There must be ample room for both parties to be fully covered by the waters. The Patriarch dunks his editor. Now Brother Eugene, in my stead, could act as the Patriarch's scribe.

"Go fetch me one of my Sappington's pills. I feel a fever coming on," I order the malleable, hateful Sister Nona. "I need this fever softened. I cannot be baptized for my Mother without one."

I take the offered pill from Sister Nona without water and plunge immediately into the pool. I had asked the Patriarch to perform the ceremony when next in the saintly city. I go into the water for my Mother's soul, baptized vicariously by her saintly proxy into Mormonism. Thus is my Mother given a chance at full Salvation. I know that my Mother's baptism is urgent. I feel that my foremother anxiously awaits complete ordinances on her behalf. Spirits cannot perform their own ordinances. They must rely on the intervention of one of the Latter Day Saints as their deputy.

I catch the vain Sister Sarah looking on, smiling at this assembly line of proxies. Hateful Shoshone.

"The worthy dead thus become heirs of the fullness of the Father's kingdom," the Patriarch says simply as he enters the pool to administer the baptismal. He lets the waters flow over both of

CHAPTER EIGHT

us. He dunks me once more and brings me again to the surface.

I gasp for air. I shudder all over. I cannot gain my breath. I see clearly the mansions of the blessed. I have no need to fear Death, the haggard porter whose feeble spell is trumped by God. "To the dying, death is kind," I blurt out. "I rejoin the Prophet Joseph, sealed to him in Celestial Heaven."

The Patriarch lifts me, his baptismal charge, out of the Fount.

I gasp for breath.

The Patriarch shakes himself off and speaks. "The Earth shall disclose her blood, and shall no more cover the slain." Is this my Mother he is addressing or me?

I look at the Patriarch closely. "I will not live to see your Prophet-hood. Trust only those that will help you."

I hear the Patriarch's voice faintly, "If this be death, you are the slain daughter of my people. God hath rendered his harvest complete. It is just as important to die as to be born, for the spirit to leave the body as for it to enter the body."

The words are stopping. I cannot hear their solace. I cannot...

CHAPTER NINE

Brother Eugene

JULY 24, 1862
SALT LAKE CITY, THE TABERNACLE

Sister Prudence gasped for air but could find none. She shook violently and then became still.

I, now fully Brother Eugene, looked on: a Mormon but ever the journalist intrigued by death.

The Patriarch looked around as if he were personally threatened. "My pen will not be stayed by my enemies," he spoke to Sister Prudence's corpse. "We are made more perfect by your example, you who were the recorder and the helpmate of Prophets. Sister Prudence, your death, regardless of cause, is but a minor footnote in this Latter Day wickedness. You are bound for Celestial Times to mingle with the worthy dead and to peacefully wait, safe in infinite atonement, for the resurrection. I will visit you there, in the presence of your true husband, the Prophet Joseph, when God is ready for me. Then we shall all be joint-heirs with Christ in the fullness of the Father's kingdom."

The Patriarch, the baptismal fount himself, uninterested in the

CHAPTER NINE

Death that surrounded him, continued to drip dry.

Must I, now Brother Eugene, anointed as scribe, accepted as a son, act the detective alone?

If I must be a detective again, I must transcend the barriers of my waking self.

JULY 26, 1862
SWEETVILLE

We, one wife less, journeyed quickly back to Sweetville.

"First Sister Karita, then Sister Willa's child, now Sister Prudence. Death does not come with such coincidence," I told Brother Port and Doctor Peter.

I certainly could not trust the unbiased detecting of long-haired, dead shot Brother Port. He was Brigham's emissary and spy pure and simple. Wherever the carpenter Prophet sent him, so he would follow. Whenever the Prophet spoke, all debate was over. Doctor Peter was more helpful, but he was tied up in whatever had been between him and Sister Karita. How could he, in grief, find a murderer?

"There is something noxious in this family. Something that threatens them all," Peter said.

"I would look to the murderous Shoshone, Sister Sarah," Brother Port interjected. "She brought the tea to Sister Karita and held Sister Willa's boy before he died. I have heard she was not happy that Sister Willa had a male child. Perhaps she killed him. She could be poisoning them. Does she not gather poisons with her brother, Twin Spirit?"

"But what of Sister Prudence's death?" I asked.

"Who knows what that Sappington pill contained?" Brother Port answered.

"But they were brought by Sister Nona," I reported.

"Shoshone are tricky enough to substitute one pill for another. Sister Nona was but the emissary," he observed. "The Shoshone are saucy and overbearing. The Patriarch caters to them, protects them, but they are like vipers. Sister Sarah is a snake let loose amongst us."

"And her brother, Twin Spirit, who can trust whatever sex he/she might be!" Brother Port continued. "He is a doggoned, red-bellied critter."

"But all of the wives had access," Doctor Peter countered. "Any one of them might have some motivation."

"The Shoshone hate the Mormons and are trying to get them to leave this valley. Sister Sarah has both the means and the motivation. They want to punish the Sweets. Look to them for your solution." Brother Port dismissed me.

The two left the porch of the Patriarch's house. I remained alone, pondering the dynamics of a family that might engender this series of murders. If everything has to do with family, where was I with my failed parentage—I who had had no glorious, bright-eyed, romping childhood? Where was I with my problematic attempt at marriage—I, who was now bunking alone, Abigail having moved to Abel's room? How could I understand any family?

The Patriarch approached.

"What can I do to help, Patriarch? Murder is stalking your family."

The Patriarch dismissed such trivialities. "There is no plot

CHAPTER NINE

against us. God is calling in my wives and children. He knoweth why. Come to my study tomorrow after dinner. We have more important things to discuss. I have some editing that God has assigned to you, my son, the scribe."

Brother Evan, the eldest son, arrived. I was supposed to meet him there. He was taking me to a Shoshone ceremony that night. Abel, ever on the lookout for the picturesque, had asked to go also.

"Where are you headed, son?"

"I have promised to take Brother Eugene and the painter to view the Shoshone festivities tonight. It is the festival of the ma ai'pots."

"But that ceremony be the ways of the Devil. Twin Spirit will be there cavorting. That creature shows the mark of the Devil."

"Father, do you forbid me to go?"

"No, as your Bishop I advise against going. You are free enough to decide your own fate."

"Then I will go. There are some things a fella can't keep himself from doing. And it is important to show these Easterners the ways of the Shoshone."

The Patriarch dismissed us as if we were beneath his purview.

JULY 26, 1862
CACHE VALLEY

The warriors sprinkled sacred cornmeal on the ground in preparation. Rattles sounded from within the lodge announcing the start of the festivities. Three warriors with feathered drums hunkered down around Twin Spirit. Two warriors with rattles joined them. Four sets of twelve warriors came out of the Medicine Lodge, nearly naked, painted with white clay.

Twin Spirit began to chant. The wind seemed to sing its response from the nearby cliffs. A pack of coyotes called, piercing his chant.

"He is welcoming the Great Spirit. He is explaining how the Spirit will come quickly to show the light," Brother Evan translated for us.

I was attracted by the freedom of Twin Spirit's chanting. He spoke. "Everyone makes his feast as he thinks best, to please the Great Spirit, who has the care of all beings created. All are of one blood, made by the same hands, and filled with the essence of the Great Mystery. The Great Spirit is here at this feast, not as an onlooker but in each movement of our dance. He dances through us."

The drumming and rattling picked up rhythmically. The warriors, stripped to their jutting strings, paired off, and began to dance. As each warrior danced, he thrust forward his scalp-laden lance. Each pair kept a jarring, shuffling step. They danced in groups of twelve. The rattlers and the drummers were untiring.

Twin Spirit shed his warrior/squaw garments and donned an outfit of feathers. He was the ma ai'pots, and as such, lance-less. He joined the dancers, in sequence each group of twelve, and all circled around him. He danced with a peculiar jarring step, waving a decorated pipe and shaking a rattle. Twin Spirit carried within himself the Great Spirit. He was fully cognizant of his centrality. I marveled at his assurance.

Who was the truer Prophet, Patriarch Sweet or Twin Spirit? The Patriarch had the clearer aspiration to speak for the Lord. He

CHAPTER NINE

wished to be the new Joseph Smith. But Twin Spirit effortlessly received the Great Spirit. Twin Spirit lived in a magic world, not unlike the Patriarch and Joseph Smith. The Patriarch was writing a book, while Twin Spirit embodied his own story.

Abel was quickly catching each set piece in hurried sketches. Diving, bobbing, careening in supplication to the Great Spirit, all was there to be captured by Abel's pen.

Twin Spirit came over to Brother Evan and circled him with his feathers.

"Brother Evan, I am not marked off. Come dance with me and find yourself."

Twin Spirit touched Evan and seemed to infuse him with new energy. Evan left Abel and me alone. Evan removed his shirt and bare to the waist began to dance.

At first Twin Spirit danced mockingly as if playing the fool. He was a jester making fun of the reserve of Evan's movement. I joined in the laughter. But then Evan caught the rhythms and the two danced as if they were a pair. Evan began hopping around like a rabbit freeing himself of his Mormon constraints. His face took on the countenance of the reborn. He became for this moment part Shoshone.

Even Abel, an artist of self-nomination, not of calling, could not miss the drama of this conversion. He moved away from me to get a better angle for another sketch. The ma ai'pots dance, even sketched without animation, was a subject worthy of great poets or painters. Abel's finished picture would not be the dance of the ma ai'pots. It would be a pale, quaint representation with an illusion of space and movement designed for New York City eyes, for New

York City sale. The picture, hung safely on the wall, would fade, but I would remember the freedom of the dance throughout my days.

Twin Spirit smiled at me and gestured to one of the other warriors who was not dancing to join me. The warrior presented himself before me, gestured with his lance, as firm an invitation as at a ceremonial ball. Perhaps Twin Spirit thought I was like Evan, ready to be regenerated. I was unsure what to do but, somewhat reluctantly, shook my head. I did not want to be caught in some Abel sketch. Twin Spirit sent the warrior away. The ma ai'pots smiled at me. He seemed to know I was not ready to publicly dance.

Twin Spirit and Evan began to dance faster now as the sweat formed on Evan's bare chest. The look he had on his face was frighteningly intense. The dance moved into the shadows of the fire. Evan and Twin Spirit were encircled by first one group, then another. It was as if the dance was encircling their very souls. Evan seemed less a Mormon lad, more a Shoshone warrior. They danced together as one. Surely they were a far better coupling than I was with my ill-fitted spouse, Abigail.

I remembered the two men dancing at that bar in New York when I was researching the Whitman phrenology murders. Surely those Charlotte Anns with their more masculine partners were less well-paired than this matched set.

A clown dancer sporting a huge artificial penis came into the dancers, mocking the way Twin Spirit and Evan were dancing. Everyone, except Abel, laughed. It was very humorous to make fun of sex, and I was much taken with this freedom. That fun was what I missed in my infrequent, mistimed dalliances with Abigail. Humorless, they had a hostile, deathlike seriousness.

CHAPTER NINE

Abel sneered and sketched furiously with new props to incorporate.

The dance stopped. Everyone slowed down and relaxed. A handsome, sacred pipe of red stone was passed from one panting warrior to another.

Evan and Twin Spirit joined me, including me in their conversation. Evan kept his Mormon shirt off. The two did not seem to care that they had a non-Shoshone observer. They used a halting, breathless English.

"Warrior have ma ai'pots wife lucky. Mormon have multiple wives. Ma ai'pots have multiple warriors. I bed each in turn. Unholy for me to lie with squaw. Not what Great Spirit wants," Twin Spirit flirted.

"I never thought much of having a Mormon God. If He be ag'in you and me, then I guess I no longer cater to Him," Evan countered.

"Don't stay Mormon. Come be Shoshone."

"I reckon I could think about it. With you I'm more myself. But can I aim that high?"

"All connected. I take your pain."

"I laugh with joy to be around you. I'm a rainbow coming alive."

"My heart, an aspen leaf, shivers."

"Answers come before questions."

"I make sweat lodge so you find Great Spirit. Come, warrior, come."

"When I am ready."

Twin Spirit left the two of us alone.

Thankfully Abel was still sketching. How much of Evan and Twin Spirit's love dialogue had he heard? Why was I so taken by its passion?

Evan turned to me and said, "I find in my times with Twin Spirit that I am a better man than I thought. He gives me a chance at something. It's not just lust, it's something rounder."

Abel looked me over as Evan was leaving. He continued sketching with a half-smile on his face.

Each man, longing for others, must rise up from solitude, and in the midst of his fellow creatures, accept his tragic aloneness. For only then can he who has found himself, seek out his brothers. Evan had almost committed himself and seemed to have found something. But what of me, life's errant detective?

I did not sleep much that evening. I certainly did not focus on detection. The murders, be they two or three, had to wait. I was too riled up by what I had seen and what I had felt. I was sleeping alone, Abigail-less once more. She had gone to Abel's room, perhaps permanently, without comment. I turned to the wall striving for sleep.

I heard a commotion outside of riders going past, then shouting. I gave up and went outside. Two groups of a dozen Shoshone were on a raid stealing horses. Perhaps I was imagining it, but I thought I recognized the warrior that had caused me such consternation by inviting me to dance. I marveled at his assurance.

The warriors stole some twenty horses. I watched, torn between fear and admiration. The Mormons ran after the Shoshone raiders but without success.

JULY 27, 1862
SWEETVILLE

In recompense for the nighttime raid, Chief Sagwitch was arrested

CHAPTER NINE

with a half-dozen of the elder Shoshone and brought to the Patriarch's house. For his own safekeeping, or so the Patriarch claimed. I arrived as the Chief was led up the front porch to the Patriarch.

"Why do your braves steal from the Mormons?" the Patriarch asked. "We are sent here to be your protectors."

"You steal valley. Indian no sleep now, no potato, no wheat, no beef. Our children are laid by the stone to be eaten by wolves. We starve. We want make good farm."

"You must trust us. We will yet find a permanent garden for you, descendants of Lemuel. We will call it Lemuel's Garden."

"This garden is the garden of our ancestors. We stay here."

"No. Cache Valley is willed by the Lord to Zion for Mormon settlement. You must learn to live at a suitable distance from the white settlers. I will lead you into a reservation to the north where you will be safe to plow and make wheat for your suffering families."

"Why we go?"

"Because God has willed it. In time He will see to you. After you have converted in the spirit to the Church of the Latter Day Saints, you will be saved by the hundreds and thousands. All will be baptized. All will seek the truthful light of the Mormon gospel. Trust me, for I am the chosen one, the rightful successor of the Prophets. I will protect the Shoshone."

A shot resounded. Where it came from was not clear. Who shot? Who were they aiming at?

Sagwitch slumped over and fell bleeding in the leg. The Patriarch looked shocked. Was he a target? I reached down to help Chief Sagwitch.

The front door slammed open. Sister Sarah emerged from the house.

"Leave my father to me!" Sister Sarah shouted as her White Cloud side came to the fore. She ran into the house and returned with bandages. "Why, Tekwahi? Why did you come here to this darkened place down below?"

"I came to hear of trust from your Patriarch," the Chief answered slowly.

"Trust," she mocked. "A Shoshone can no more trust a Mormon than a Sister can have belief in her Patriarch."

She turned to the Patriarch. "I will take my father inside and nurse him in the Blue Room. At least there you Mormons might not stalk him. Send for the doctor."

Sister Sarah took her father away from the bloodied scene into the Patriarch's house.

The Patriarch looked around, for once speechless.

"Who did this?" I asked angrily. "Some Mormon?"

"Not one that follows his Bishop," he answered firmly.

"And who does not follow his Bishop?"

"Spies sent by bogus Prophets."

"Brother Port?"

"Make of it what you will, detective!" the Patriarch taunted me. He had regained his full composure. "But enough of these idle mysteries, we have work to do."

"Come editor," he said, leading me into the safety of his study. "I have the Lord's Word to show you."

JULY 27, 1862
SWEETVILLE, THE PATRIARCH'S STUDY

The Patriarch stared across his paper-filled desk, looking me over as

CHAPTER NINE

if to validate my worthiness. I was not sure what message my body was giving him. Apparently I passed the test as he continued on.

"Joseph Smith entrusted the beginning of his divinely translated book to someone unworthy. Martin Harris asked three times to show them to his family. The third time, in weakness, the Prophet gave way. Harris gave the Prophet a covenant that he would return the document but his covenant was false. I ask of you a covenant."

"A covenant for what?"

"That you will help me craft the missing pages and tell no one how we did it."

"I give you, Father, my covenant."

"Once a Prophecy has been recorded, it must not be revisited."

"Have you found the missing document?"

The Patriarch paused. "No. I have been granted access to the Golden Tablets and have almost finished a new translation."

"What must I do?"

"You must make my Prophecy fit into the allotted space."

"I can help you there. Let me see the source and I will shape it to the right proportions."

"I have more work to do. It is not ready yet, but soon. Soon I will need your editing. Study the Book, for this is a prelude to it. See how it begins and imagine a preamble to it. It must seem consistent in its flow. It cannot seem like different speakers, for this be the Lord's Word."

"When can I start?"

"Soon. A day or two. My task is hard but my Prophecy must come forth."

"Will this help in your election to the Twelve?"

"Of course. For I am a true Prophet, not some mere carpenter."

"But what of your wives, their murders?"

"These episodes are mere encumbrances to tempt me away from completing my task. But the Devil will not interrupt me."

"Go... study, my scribbler son," he dismissed me. "You have divine work to be done."

I had to edit and I had to detect. Numbers, numbers, everywhere I turned there were numbers. One hundred sixteen pages to count and craft. The Patriarch, one of the Seventy, who had aspirations to be of the Twelve and then of the Three and then the One. Eight wives, of which the seventh, Sister Karita, and the fifth, Sister Prudence, were no more. Both murders were of the odd-numbered wives. Was that the insight that fit to this story? If so, then were not the other odd-numbered wives in jeopardy? I had to look out for Sister Hannah and Mother Evangeline.

Be it as the scribe or as the detective, I had to search out the solution that was most fitting.

CHAPTER TEN

✂—

The Testimony of Sister Nona, Fourth Wife

JULY 28, 1862
SWEETVILLE

I tend the front garden. I am safest with the earth. Alone. Sister-less. Here, not in all the tomes of Mormonism, is my salvation. Here, in this garden, there is respite from the carking pain that has me ponder suicide as some long-lost friend. Here I am safe, away from the dwindling crowd of Sisters. Here I forget the wrongness of my essential nature, the choice I had forced upon me by an assuming Patriarch, that decision that gave me an inward pollution that hath no remedy. Here there is the illusion of irrigation for my spring-less soul.

I have never known how to mimic a merry heart. Not as a child in Wales. Not as the simple bride of Brother Mark. Certainly never as part of this harem of Sisterdom. I cannot smile to feign contentment. Though I get solace from gardening, still I cannot live a single day without finding the world remote, strange, sinister, and uncanny.

Once back in that house, even in the supposed safety of the Blue

Room, I am made infirm by the shadows of my abode. I begrudge Sister Katherine the assuredness of her sunny disposition. I cannot stomach Sister Willa with her purposefulness. The Shoshone is too full of liveliness. Everywhere within this house there are inlets of dark, apprehensive fear. I live for months sunk in this prison house, surrounded by noisy Sisters, lethargic, without belief or hope. I am like a coarse carcass reddened by my habit of misery. Everything, even our Mormon God, lacks the taste and zest of spring.

Then for a moment, at last outside in the suckling storm, I relish the burgeoning earth and escape for just one moment my pining, mumping mood.

But I am not allowed to stay alone. Brother Eugene approaches to ask more questions.

"Why are you called Sister Nona?" the probing Brother Eugene asks me without greeting. I do not feel safe talking to this Yankee Gentile who claims to have joined us. Though there is hardly a touch of threatening maleness about him, still I do not trust him.

"I was the ninth child my mother birthed back in Wales. Nona means nine. She said she gave me that name for good luck."

"Did it grant you good luck?"

"Never."

"But are not your days ever bright?" he interrogates me.

"My eyes see the gloomy side. Lost in an unhappiness that is mean and ugly. Men have forced me to do things I did not want to do."

"You mean the Patriarch forcing you to his bed?"

"That is part of the bargain."

"What bargain is that?"

CHAPTER TEN

"You ask too many questions, Brother Eugene. I feel that you are taking it all in and will spit me out as a character in some Mormon novel."

"You can trust me, Sister Nona. I just want to know everything about this family. I need each Sister's story. It might help in understanding what is happening to this family."

"I have no role in that. I have only my two daughters. I only want my daughters to find accountable men who choose to have a single wife. Not for them, this multi-headed monster of a family. This wretched Sisterdom. Meanwhile I'm of the Blue Room."

"Blue Room? What do you mean by that?"

"Haven't all the murders had to do with the Gold Room? Sister Karita, Sister Prudence."

"But what of Sister Willa's son? He died in the Blue Room."

"That may have been a murder or it could just be the Mormon God's will. If that was murder, than it also was a Gold Room killing."

"How so?"

"Because if the son had lived, then Sister Willa would have been made Celestial. She would then have moved to the Gold Room."

"Do you miss Sister Karita and Sister Prudence?"

"Miss them!" I need no longer tolerate the silver blissfulness of Sister Karita, nor listen to the constant, unsolicited advice of Sister Prudence. "Hardly. It is quieter without them."

"So you feel safe in the Blue Room?"

"I am as safe as one can be in this household."

"But do you not want to be Celestially bound to the Patriarch? Do you not want to be fated for the heaven where he will reside?"

"No. I have seen enough of the Patriarch. Our time on Earth

has been quite enough."

I try to leave the writer/detective pondering my insights, but he will not let me alone. I try to resume tending the front garden, but Brother Eugene still has questions. He must know how I decided to join this house, how I became part of this Sisterdom.

I don't really remember deciding to join but I must have.

AUGUST 8, 1844
SUCCESSION BATTLE, NAUVOO, ILLINOIS

Our leaders converged on comely Nauvoo to plan what to do next. Joseph Smith was dead. We were leaderless. We had to make the pretense of choosing direction. And with this as background, I had to also choose between two husbands. Two questions, two selections that had to be certified. As if I or we had the possibility of choice.

A tired Brother Sidney Rigdon had returned to Nauvoo from ill-fated political electioneering in Pennsylvania five days earlier. He rose to speak. He claimed he was "the identical man that the ancient Prophets had sung about, wrote and rejoiced over; and that he was sent to do the identical work that had been the theme of all the Prophets in every preceding generation." He threatened our enemies that their "blood would be to the horses bridles." His message, though a bit incoherent in speech, remained clear. He, an ordained Prophet and the surviving member of the First Presidency, held Joseph's keys. He must be anointed the Mormon "Guardian." He offered himself as our "Constable." It was he that called for that August 8th meeting to validate his election.

The surviving members of the Twelve Apostles sped toward

CHAPTER TEN

Nauvoo. They claimed that leadership must roll upon the shoulders of the Twelve Apostles, not the First Presidency. Which group, the Twelve or the Three, was given the charge? Brother Brigham, arriving from Boston, reported a dream of being given the "Keys to the Kingdom." As leader of the Apostles, Brother Brigham felt he had the power to be or at least to name the successor. He wrote us in a letter that "When God sends a man to do a work, all the devils in hell cannot kill him until he gets through his work."

Brother Sidney Rigdon and Brother Brigham Young were not the only candidates talked about in those confusing days. Hyram Smith, an obvious successor, had been murdered with the Prophet. Samuel Smith, a younger brother of the Prophet, had died at the end of July of natural causes. Mother Emma, the Prophet's widow, favored William Marks as a "trustee in trust" until her young son could take over. William Smith, another of Joseph's brothers, was a possible candidate, although he was considered unreliable.

Many possibilities for our Church, but I was caught up in my own dilemma. I was married to a fellow Welsh native, Mark Roberts, and with him had come to America, eventually to Nauvoo. Brother Mark was a good man but twistable. My proud husband bragged often to the congregation about my virtue and my willingness to follow orders. When our Bishop John Sweet had sent Brother Mark to preach in far away Palestine, he had promised Brother Mark that he would look out for me. I still do not know if my husband knew the implications of the Bishop's plan. I was taken into the Bishop's house with Mother Evangeline, Sister Katherine, and Sister Hannah. This was before Sister Prudence, though slotted, joined the Sisterdom.

Why had Brother Mark, who had vowed to keep me safe, left

me here in the Patriarch's house? Why was he so gullible as to think me safe here amongst a growing harem of women, each subservient to this horned Patriarch? Ordered to go on missionary duty, did he not see that ministering to me, protecting me, was his ultimate mission?

Brother Mark and I had not had any children. God had not blessed our union yet. We were like two Welsh children lost in the woods. Only two, without sin.

I heard the Patriarch coming that first night. I expected him. He did not speak at first. He did not ask. He assumed that a bedded woman in his house was his by Providence.

I shook my head violently. I shouted out, "Stop!" He paid me no heed.

I wailed, "Leave me alone. I am not yours."

Mother Evangeline came to the door and calmly said, "Do not cry out. Let the other Sisters sleep. You cannot deny him."

"But..." I moaned.

"Once it starts there are no buts," she answered. "Hush up."

He raised my nightdress. Hands, hands everywhere.

I tightened my legs at the hips. I would not let him soil me. He placed his hand over my mouth and scissored at my knees to overcome me. I tightened back. He was so strong. The strength of Prophets.

"You are fated to be mine." His only words that night. Without passion. Without question. Allowing no answer.

My hips weakened against his assurance.

He opened his bedclothes. I shut my eyes. If I did not look, it would not be happening. I froze up within.

CHAPTER TEN

He hurt me that night as he spilled his seed. Every night since, the same pain. I must stay strong. I must hide my wounded weakness.

I awoke the next morn numb, sure of what had happened but dazed. I remembered through a series of curtains, each deeper within me.

I hated seeing the other Sisters. Sister Hannah, with her tongues, made my head spin. Sister Katherine, with her songs of saintliness, rankled. Mother Evangeline, with her calmness, made me rage internally. The visits of Sister Prudence, awash in words, annoyed me. I avoided them, these wanton, soiled Sisters.

If the Patriarch entered the room, I could not look at him. His assurance was an emblem of my despair.

He came to my room every fourth night then. No words. No crying out. Deadly consistency. I spent each day counting nights. Knowing when he would next come. When I would have to choose again not to choose. When the terror would happen again. Every fourth day I was speechless.

Mother Evangeline spoke to me, "You will get used to it. It is whatever it is. It shall be your burden." I knew I never would get used to it. I searched for a way out.

Now I was noticeably betrayed in pregnancy, facing childbirth with its feigned hopefulness.

"You must marry me now or face eternal damnation," the Patriarch argued. "In me you will find the fullness of exaltation."

"But what of Brother Mark?" How could I, soiled, reunite with Brother Mark, my former fellow child? Was not childhood past?

The Patriarch scoffed at my feigning decision. Of course the decision had been his as a Prophet of his preeminent God.

"I will take him aside when he returns," he said. "I will tell him that the woman he claims for a wife does not belong to him. That you are my spiritual wife as granted by the God of Mormon. I am your proxy. You and our future children are my property. Brother Mark can go where he pleases, and get another wife, but he must be sure to get one of his allotted spirits."

"Have I no choice?" I asked lamely, knowing that choice, if I ever had a choice, was that first night. It had been overcome.

"No. We are bound spiritually. Our child is a talisman. My fate is your fate."

"What if I left?"

"If you abandon me, you abandon the Mormon Church. You will be a whore cast out."

"And what will that make you?"

"Me? I remain a Prophet finding his spiritual wives."

I did not answer him then. Though I knew I could not choose another option that I did not have. I turned to the wall in silence.

It was mid-morning when the Patriarch, Mother Evangeline, Sister Katherine, Sister Hannah, the assigned-but-not-yet-wed Sister Prudence, and my rudderless self went to listen to Elder Sidney Rigdon speak. There was a healthy wind blowing and his speech was hard to hear and harder to follow. He climbed to a wagon, but still we could not hear him. Many shouted for him to talk louder. He said something about ending "the hidden sin of polygamy." At least that was what the Patriarch claimed to have heard, but who could tell? I listened as if in a trance.

I am sure that Biblical and Mormon scripture was quoted. Elder

CHAPTER TEN

Rigdon claimed the "mantle of revelation." He must have talked about Isaiah. But then we Mormons rattle on about Prophets without end. It was like the ranting of an elderly, worn-out lunatic. He jabbered on for well nigh an hour-and-a-half. In the end how can anyone know what he said? At least the Patriarch did his abominations silently.

Hundreds attended, anxious to know the direction our Church might take. The crowd started to murmur like a leaderless flock of sheep. If this be our future bedrock, what sustenance could we find? Some left, in a muddle. I, husbandless, leaderless, remained untethered.

Rigdon, for he was no longer Elder to me, sputtered to an end. Someone shouted, "We must take a vote."

"Vote for what?"

"Elect a Prophet!"

The crowd grumbled, unsure.

It was then that Brother Brigham mounted the makeshift podium decisively. He talked briefly, sharply, clearly.

"I will manage this vote for Elder Rigdon. He does not preside here. I, but a child, will manage this flock for a season. It is not a time for a hurrying spirit. There must be a true organization of our Church. Let us meet today at two o'clock to decide what next to do."

The flock, spoken to clearly, left calmed. But the Patriarch turned to us angrily. "Who does that carpenter think he is? In whose name does he speak?"

By two o'clock we Sisters had seats to the right in the General Assembly. I chose to sit with them, so I must be one of them. Had I, who had no room for decision, decided? We feign to act and by our actions choose.

The Patriarch sat on the left in the rear with the lesser priesthood. He was not then trusted enough to be one of the Seventy. Rigdon's followers gathered around him on the stand. Nearby the Apostles mounted their numbers. The Assembly started late.

I remember most the wind and how difficult it was to hear. My ill-fated marriage path was in the air, but somehow it blended with the question of our Church. Sisterdom beckoned with its wan expectation of contentment. What was next? Who? Everything was incoherent. The quiet rage of decisions.

"We are leaderless," Brother Brigham took the lead. "We have all done the best we could. Now we must walk by faith and not by sight until we can find our way. The Twelve Apostles, chosen by revelation, will lead the way out of the darkness. The Twelve Apostles will ordain the Prophet. Look to us for guidance. To choose another path, to elect in passion without considered thought, will sever all." He was sure that Elder Rigdon was not the chosen course. In that he was forceful. He, with a carpenter's assurance, was a manly leader. He assumed leadership over us.

Elder Rigdon looked to his supporters for sustenance. He was practically speechless, too tired from his morning harangue to argue again. Those chosen to speak for him prevaricated and recanted. His candidacy, which this morning had seemed possible, flickered and died. He seemed less a Prophet, more an old, bald, broken-down man.

The Assembly was pleased to cede the decision to the Apostles. We were silent. Everyone knew that meant Brother Brigham, but at least we did not have to decide that now. Let our right of decision

CHAPTER TEN

be abrogated.

The Patriarch was not happy with the ascendancy of Brother Brigham. "A mere carpenter can never become a true Prophet."

The Patriarch flirted with the idea of leaving Nauvoo for the wilds of Pennsylvania with Elder Rigdon. Perhaps this schism might have more leadership opportunities for someone under a cloud like the Patriarch. But Elder Rigdon was not supportive of polygamy. Might the Patriarch choose Rigdon and lose his growing Sisterdom? Impossible. We were his.

Brother Brigham had the clear support of the majority. We let him decide for us. We Mormons abandoned the unfinished Nauvoo Temple and followed Brother Brigham westward.

And I, who sat with the bound Sisterdom, who loathed the Patriarch who had defiled me, who was without choice, followed.

JULY 28, 1862
SWEETVILLE

"And that was the illusion I had and the Mormons had. Of choice." I finish telling my story to ever-listening Brother Eugene. I look up to find Sister Sarah, Twin Spirit, and Brother Evan by our side.

"What of the other Sisters who joined after you?" Brother Eugene asked. "Do not they lighten your burden?"

"The harem of Sisters expands. Each in turn I pity and I hate. Another wanton Sister who does not cry out is no succor. Their names, their countenances, barely register. Though the fourth night frequency lessens, still I count each day. Still that nightly horror beckons."

"We have no alternatives," Sister Sarah muses. "I, who was some treaty between the Chief and the Patriarch, know that only too well."

"Life just happens to us Sisters," I continue with resignation. "We are decision-less. We have not fallen from grace, for a fall implies intention. Some call it fate but that implies a higher plan. There is no plan, just the endless obligation of penitent Sisterdom."

Twin Spirit places his hand gently on the shoulder of Brother Evan. "The Great Spirit is freedom. Each of us has a time when we must decide. We live the life we choose."

Brother Evan, the Patriarch's eldest son, a man who might decide, nods quietly.

"Perhaps men can choose, but we Sisters are sentenced for eternity," I add bitterly. "We are taken. The Patriarch is our lot. We are his promised ones."

"Shouldn't we just flee? Leave him," Sister Sarah asks me defiantly.

"Flee? To other assuming men? To other deciders? Would that be an improvement? At least I know what to expect from this Patriarch. Life once done in cannot be righted. We must accept it as our lot."

"Is there no escape?" Brother Eugene asks.

"The only escape is in the destruction of the Sisterdom," I answer.

CHAPTER ELEVEN

Brother Eugene

JULY 29, 1862
SWEETVILLE

We dined at the Patriarch's on pancakes with molasses and supped on biscuits made of flour ground in Evan's mill, butter, dried beef, peach-sauce, and custard pie. Abel filled himself with sweets, expanding his girth. Abigail studied Abel as if his ampleness promised a bribe for her allegiance. Abigail eyed this smoothed out, touched up, plentiful man, so hardy next to my unmanly thinness. Abigail had journeyed with Abel and me to Utah, but possibly had already known her direction before she had left. And I was not it. I may have been left behind before our journey even began. I discovered I did not care.

The Patriarch argued baldly against the unspoken contract between Abigail and Abel. "The Lord is impatient with flagrant, hideous adultery. A clean woman cannot be attracted to he who is unclean. Beware, adulteress, ye that have located your fellow adulterer. I offer you instead a way to sainthood. Where there once was eight, there can be nine. Three times three, a trinity."

Mother Evangeline tried to rise, but the Patriarch motioned harshly for her to remain sitting. She said snappishly, "You cannot protect your existing wives and yet you, of all people, talk about adding a ninth. You who cannot protect your existing sons seek more."

"The Lord's ways are not mysterious. Our family is formed out in the open."

He continued to direct his plea to Abigail. "I offer you instead a way to sainthood."

Sister Sarah spoke up vehemently. "Yes, come join this vanishing family in its wretched saintliness." I observed her bitterness. Was it a strong enough motive for murder?

The Patriarch continued to address my wife, "I offer you a way out from your simpering indifference."

I, Brother Eugene, a scribe, a son, listened to the Patriarch solicit my wife.

Abigail smiled coquettishly. "Patriarch, you flatter me with such attention."

He would not be put off. "I do not tempt you by calling you beautiful, for such words are a deadly poison. I see that you can only attain your true beauty when you have joined me as my ninth wife."

"And would I sleep in that emptying chamber, the Gold Room?" Abigail taunted him. "Or must I birth you a son first?"

Abigail laughed as if she alone were privy to a great joke. She was not threatened by the Patriarch's attentions. She would not be bound by this closed room conspiracy with its threat of captivity. Even if she were to agree—and I knew she would not—she would barter her own terms. She would join neither the Blue nor the Gold

CHAPTER ELEVEN

Room. She would negotiate her own space wherein she would reign triumphant.

"Repent of your deep-dyed sins. You are keeping Spirits from being born. You are dammed up not allowing your false husband's seed to flower." The Patriarch waved his hand at me dismissively. "I am here to show you the way. Walk while ye still have the light and find the gates of Zion, lest darkness come upon you."

Abigail listened closely, as if weighing the Patriarch's tempting words. She flirted with this mesmerizing man, making light of his offerings of marriage. She seemed to savor the whimsy of playing this scene before the Sisters, her husband, and her lover.

"What if I were to choose to be childless?"

"With me as a spouse, you would not long be childless."

"And without you as spouse?"

"You will reap only disappointment. You will be alone in the endlessness of eternity."

"Well at least I can have my own bedroom," Abigail laughed hysterically. She and Abel rose together. "Come, Abel. You have some sketching to do."

"Stay, scribe. We have work to do." I followed the Patriarch into his study.

JULY 29, 1862
SWEETVILLE, THE PATRIARCH'S STUDY

"The loss of the one hundred sixteen pages was Satan's attempt to sully the mission of the Prophet Joseph Smith. I am charged with their recovery," the Patriarch began.

I asked how the pages were lost.

"Martin Harris was helping to copy and edit the first section of the Book. He asked three times to borrow the opening section to show to his family. On the third request, Joseph weakened and let him take the manuscript."

I asked why the Mormon Lord had allowed Joseph to be misled.

"Because the Lord had to show Joseph the cunning ways of Satan. He also had to demonstrate to Joseph that He was all knowing and that His ends could not be frustrated. The Prophet Joseph and his wife Emma had a stillborn male child who died around this time. The Lord punishes and anoints in strange ways."

I asked what became of the one hundred sixteen pages.

"We do not know." He paused. "Probably Harris's harlot of a wife, Lucy, burned them. She showed them to a number of her relatives. Harris fought hard to regain the Prophet's trust. He was one of the Three Witnesses that attested to the truth of the Golden Plates."

I asked why the Prophet Joseph did not just retranslate the one hundred sixteen pages.

"He saw this as a plot by Satan to discredit him if the translation was not the same as the original. Satan would have the original resurface and the translations would differ."

I thought hard for my next question. "Then how can the missing pages be rediscovered?"

"A new Prophet must discover again the tablets and retranslate them in a way that is fitting."

I asked what the content was in these pages. He recounted how the Prophet Joseph said it was the Book of Lehi, a tale of how the tribe came to America. He replaced the content with a brief abridg-

CHAPTER ELEVEN

ment in the Book of Nephi. When Joseph began the Book of Nephi, he had a new scribe, Oliver Cowdery. Having found his correct scribe, the writing flowed smoothly and quickly. "That is what I ask of you: to be my chosen scribe, my Oliver Cowdery," he ended.

"So the missing pages should relate to Nephi but not match it," I offered. "They should be similar but not be the same. They should expand slightly the story."

"Yes, a different Prophet, a different scribe, composing a preamble."

"I have read again the Book of Nephi. I think I understand what might precede it. If you trust me, Patriarch, I will answer this noble charge."

"You must see the structure as a whole and then you can begin."

"But for that, I need to see what you have translated."

He looked at me doubtfully. "Can I trust you, Brother Eugene? I have seen your light-mindedness. You are a writer and are adept at taking dictation from Satan. You cavort with the Devil and his worm lives in you. Can you escape the cynical indifference of this sectarian, writer's world?"

"But that was before, Patriarch." I said what was expected, believing it. "Through you and your ministry, I have seen the way. I am ready to repent, walk up rightly, and sin not."

"I know of your hashish habit. How you searched for it in Salt Lake to debase your soul."

"But that was before. Now my body is baptized to the temple of God."

"The Lord told me He would send me a scribe who I must first sanctify and then use his service to speed along my work. And you have come," he convinced himself.

He needed a writer whose language was copious, fluent in utterance, with articulation clear and musical. He needed a scribe that would follow him wherever the Lord in a shower of language taketh. I was that scribe. A worthy son of a worthy father.

"I cannot hold back the Word. I am weary from holding it in, I must let it go forth. Together we shall find the words, eat them, and regurgitate them as Prophecy."

He bid me get down again on my knees.

"I give you the Word, as a Prophet's scribe, my son, Brother Eugene."

With that the Patriarch asked me to rise and made the sign of the cross over me.

"Take them." He shunted some scribbled pages at me. I noticed that the Patriarch had finished stacks of pages. He only gave me the first stack. He must be composing through the night with an acute, measureless fever. Where did he get the content? What was the source of his revelation? "Here is the first part. Cry, son of man. I offer you respite from your brittle exile. No longer a fearful hanger-on, I offer you assurance and unification."

"But, Brother Eugene, protect these words. There are those that would find these words and destroy them," he admonished.

"Protect them from whom?"

"There are spies and murderers about us. You know that."

I was to be author of another's words, freed from the need to construct a language and tale of my own. I was not called to write a novel but to write Prophecy. This was my higher mission.

I had been a man of many words, but each past word had been

CHAPTER ELEVEN

a mockery. My songs had been filled only with anguish. My prose had echoed with longing based on my incompleteness. I, who had been caught in the grim present, futureless, unable to renew my own strength, was strong.

I felt the Patriarch's power and self-assurance. I trusted him as a Father.

I slept soundly that night alone. I was a scribe.

JULY 30, 1862
SWEETVILLE

Abel joined me at the only table, putting the finishing touches on one of his drawings. We worked apart. I did not care that he had taken my wife, for I had the Word.

One hundred sixteen handwritten pages, telling an expanded version of the story that must follow it. If there were two hundred-plus words to the page, that would be around 25,000 words. I had before me the first part.

The nascent Chapter One of Lehi, transcribed and shortened by Mormon, began with an endless series of begets, of fathers and sons, of sons of sons going back to Joseph. The Aaronic Priest Lehi pled for a repentance of sins, for the following of the true commandments, for finding and following valid Prophets. The text bemoaned an entrenched priesthood, popular and vainglorious, that did not have the mantle of Prophecy. A true Prophet must be an enemy of this entrenched priesthood and must suffer to be tried before them. He would invoke the Prophet Isaiah and plead for cleansing.

Lehi longed for such truth, but he was too comfortable in his riches to speak out. His riches were evil, but he clung to them, the crimson, not the wool. He was given praise and glory not by everlasting God but by fickle man. He suffered, for he knew he had turned from the Lord, but he did not know how to right himself. How could he take witness against this Church, the fount of all of his riches? If he cried out, the Churchmen would rise up against him and force him into the wilderness. Must he be cast out in order to find truthfulness?

I read this and thought of the Patriarch and his battles with Brother Brigham. Like Lehi, the Patriarch looked for true Prophecy, and he did not find it in the present. Brother Brigham was the rich, complacent priesthood, while the Patriarch was the Prophet, the bringer of the rebirth. One must rewrite the past in search for what was needed now. He was what was needed now. The Patriarch found in his one hundred sixteen pages a call to arms. I could not wait to read the second part.

Abel looked up from his sketch proudly. "I think I have captured the wantonness of Twin Spirit and Brother Evan well. They were pinned to each other as they danced."

I looked on. "Yes, you've caught them. Evan looks free from constraint. Be sure not to let any Mormons see your sketch."

"Maybe I should show it to his mother, the too proud Sister Hannah. That might take her down a peg." Abel rolled up his sketch and smacked his lips.

I continued to edit. I counted words, trying to fashion the material into half of the allotted pages. I realized that what I was working on was part of a campaign for the Patriarch's elevation in the Church. This was his magnum opus arguing for advancement

CHAPTER ELEVEN

first to the Twelve, the Apostles, then to the Three, the Presidency, then to his ultimate goal as lone Prophet. This preamble's goal was to elevate the Patriarch. I worked to make the text more forceful, shorter, with a more majestic ring to it. I made it worthy of a Prophet. I grew proud of my handiwork. I felt like a tool of the Lord.

CHAPTER TWELVE

The Testimony of Sister Hannah, Third Wife

JULY 30, 1862
SWEETVILLE

I hear voices from the Celestial Heaven. They speak through me, a chosen Sister, in a trustworthy tongue I do not know.

I am the third of the Patriarch's wives, but as the mother of his eldest living son, I consider myself the first without equal. I do not miss Sister Karita, for some said her beauty far outshone mine. Blissfully, Sister Willa did not birth a living son to gain entrance to the Gold Room. I do not miss Sister Prudence, for her constant lecturing and persistent recording annoyed me. Mother Evangeline is left in our room but she is harmless. Let the Gold Room empty out to the truly worthy, Celestial Heaven wives. I listen to the tongues. They tell me what to do. They keep me safe. I speak their words so that others may hear the true way to sanctity.

A successful polygamous wife must regard her husband with indifference, and with no other feeling than that of reverence, for love is that false sentiment that has no existence in Sisterdom. I belong to the Patriarch. He is my keeper.

CHAPTER TWELVE

I sleep in the Gold Room with one loaded gun at my side. It will be good for one untrustworthy Lamanite.

As I cook, I can make out the tongues in the hiss of a chunk of meat. I am sent to the Patriarch to interpret God's message through the strife of tongues. My testimony is sure, a rich treat of Adamic language. The Lord's ordinances ring true. God is here in the flesh, a close friend who converses with me directly. I know not the words, but I am sure He talks to me much of the Patriarch's gift for Prophecy.

Abel Bermann, that fattened painter, approaches me on the front porch. "Sister Hannah, I have a sketch of your son, Evan, you might like."

He unrolls it and I start, "What is Evan doing?"

"He is dancing with Twin Spirit."

"No, he is cavorting with Satan." I grab the sketch from him. I leave the porch and run to the Patriarch's study. That dreaded Shoshone Chief Sagwitch, bandaged up by his slut of a daughter, is there with the esteemed one. That untrustworthy author—the one with too many questions—the so-called Brother Eugene, is with them taking notes, spying as always.

"Look, Patriarch, look at this perfidy!" I scream. "My son, Evan, with that Shoshone harlot."

"The Devil's work!" our Patriarch shouts. "Brother Eugene, seek my son, Evan. Bring him to me, that he might face his Bishop."

"Yes, Patriarch," the spy complies.

When my renegade son joins us, he is not alone. The dreaded Twin Spirit is with him.

"Evan. How? Why?" I point to the sketch. Evan looks on stonily.

"My son, you have been led astray. You backslide," the Bishop says. How can the Patriarch be so calm?

"No, Father, I have found my own slated way."

"And that way is that of the betrayer," I sob. "Do you not hear the way that I speak quite clearly?"

"I hear mutterings, Mother, only mutterings."

I want to slap my son but cannot touch him.

The Patriarch turns to the Chief. "Your son, your so-called ma ai'pots, leads my firstborn astray."

"If a ma ai'pots comes to a family, that family must feel blessed," the Chief says calmly. "For he is a mystery the Great Spirit has created to teach us. You try to capture everything in your Prophecy, but you miss the Great Mystery."

"He dances the obscene steps of a made-up woman with a Mormon son," the Patriarch observes as our true Bishop.

"If Twin Spirit not dance with those he chooses, how could we Shoshone continue with our traditions? His freedom guarantees our religious rites. Without it no mountain, no hunt, no one worthy to lie with." The Chief spews out his untruths.

"That is why we must cordon off you Shoshone. To protect ourselves from you. To protect yourself from those who would do you harm. God does not create such blunders as ma ai'pots. They are the creation of the Devil." Our Bishop rips up the sketch and casts the remains at the sinner's feet.

The Chief is not silenced. "You threaten us, you that have an evil spirit in your wives. Protect your own wives, Patriarch. Look to the evil within your own family. Twin Spirit is not the source of your evil. I hear a coyote howling four times to bring death to your

CHAPTER TWELVE

family, Patriarch. A good man has a good home, a bad man, a bad home. Something is evil within you."

The Chief continues, "I see in Twin Spirit an echo of you, Patriarch, for are you not both a mixture of the spirit and the flesh, taking direction both from the spirit world and your own body? You fear Twin Spirit because he is a seer, like you. He too gives Prophecy."

I feel a passing wave and feel compelled to speak out. "I listen to the tongues, Patriarch. I am engorged and united with the Body of Christ. The tongue of the dumb sings. They tell me that Evan courts evil. He is no longer my son. He must be cast out. He must be punished."

The Bishop takes out his revolver, but he does not point it at Evan. "What if I were to shoot you, Brother Evan, or hang you as an apostate?"

"Father, you must do what you will, as I must do what I must. Hasn't enough of this family died from your blindness?"

Our Bishop returns his pistol to its holster. He asks questions of my no-longer son. "If you are to live, would you flee and join in refuge the Shoshone? Would you go into exile with them north of the Bear River?"

"No, I would only bring my troubles onto them."

"My sons are my hands from God. I have made you the miller, but you have defiled thy miller's hands. It is only those hands that do my bidding that can remain my sons. Those who do not must be severed at the wrist."

"Then I must go and seek my own way."

"No longer as a child of Mormon?"

"No longer as a Mormon. I will consider myself Shoshone,

although I cannot join them. I am unworthy. I will do what I can to keep the Shoshone from becoming Mormons, for that is not the way of the Great Spirit."

I speak up. "We banish you, whoremonger." I slap him across the face.

"You who never knew me cannot cast me out," Evan answers me. "I leave where I never belonged."

The Patriarch turns to the Chief, "The Devil holds such sway in this land that, not satisfied with making your son fall into so great a sin by his own self-abuse, he has made my son believe that this vice of his loins is holy. This custom began in the spirit but is now in the flesh. We, the Latter Day Saints, have been sent by the Lord to teach you that such implanted sins of the flesh must stop for the greater glory of God."

"Father, haven't you preached enough?" my ex-son asks.

Twin Spirit speaks, aiming his words at Brother Eugene, the spy, who seems to be cowering in the corner, "Be brave, writer from the East. Be brave for yourself and for this family of death. Real wisdom occurs as you give up trying to explain everything by logic. I had a spirit's dream in which I saw your murderer. The killer has a veil, is not what he or she seems to be. The killer is angry and betrayed. You must think like a murderer. Go on the warpath. Seek out the betrayed. In the ultimate betrayal, you will find the solution."

Twin Spirit turns to that unclean thing, no longer my son. "You will soon join us, Evan, as we go to this so-called reservation. There you could be a part of sacred things."

"No, Twin Spirit. I cannot, I must not. Not now. We must part. I have learned from you much about divine spirits and about myself.

I believe in you, not in the Mormon God. That must suffice."

"You will let him go!" I accuse the Patriarch. "Without proper punishment how can any of us be safe? Must I protect myself from these Lamanites? Is it not better for my son to die than for our whole Church to dwindle into unbelief?"

The Patriarch says hollowly, "His fate comes from his own judgment. We must let him go as he that is shunned. Just because he is caught doing what he ought not to do, we must not act as we ought not to act."

Once my eldest, a son no more, he does not look back as he leaves. Thankfully I have another son.

I remember the time I first heard the voices.

OCTOBER 30, 1838
HAUN'S MILL, MISSOURI

"Sister Hannah." Mother Evangeline, as ever, shouted orders to me. "I must go to the village to buy linens. Watch closely our sons." She boarded the last wagon out.

We had been warned that Missouri Governor Boggs had sent out an order that we were to be treated as enemies that must be exterminated. We were prepared, the menfolk thought. But they came so quickly.

Brother Sidney Rigdon led the complaints against those Devil's men of that dreaded state. Rigdon clamored that we were wearied of being smitten, and tired of being trampled upon. He preached that we must fight, for it is better, far better, to sleep with the dead than be oppressed among the living. He asked that our blood be atoned. He carried the seat of war to their own houses.

We warred with Missouri. Mormons raided Missouri. Missouri raided Mormons.

Of course the firebrand, Brother Sidney, was not there when Jacob Huan, the Patriarch, the menfolk, and we women and children were attacked at Haun's Mill.

A band of marauding settlers, fighting on its own hook, cornered us in that accursed Mill.

"Prepare to meet your maker, vile, invading Mormons," they cried.

The Patriarch thought that a blacksmith shop would prove a place of safety. It proved to be our slaughterhouse. It was the blasted cracks between the logs of the shop that were our undoing. The raiders picked us off like trapped cattle in an exposed pen.

"Come out, Mr. Smith," someone taunted. "Where are you? Save these Mormons. Show us an angel. Translate some more Golden Plates. Give us some more of your revelations."

At least I stayed with our threatened sons, my two, Evangeline's only one. When the Patriarch fled toward the brush, the men shot at him in derision. He made it to safety, abandoning us to our fate.

An Elder, Tom McBride, tried to call for a surrender. He exited with his arms up and threw aside his weapon. An enemy chopped him down and coolly hacked him to pieces with a corn-cutter.

I tried to cover my two sons. I heard the voices. I paused, trying to understand their message. I could not translate. I was dumbfounded. I left Evangeline's ten-year old son, William, to fend for himself.

The slaughter continued. Our men fought on until their end.

CHAPTER TWELVE

The noise of the voices saved me and my sons from our attackers.

When the Missourians detected no further movement in the shop, they came en masse. My eldest, Evan, was two. He stood proudly. Aaron, an infant, wailed. I pleaded for the life of my sons. "They are too young." The leader of the mob smirked.

William, Mother Evangeline's lone child, cowered under the bellows. One gunman laughed, "Half-grown Mormon children must be killed, for nits will make lice." Then he fired at close range, blasting the top of William's skull throughout the smithy. I covered Evan and Aaron and they somehow survived. The voices succored us.

"Enough," one killer cried. "We have taught the Mormons that they are not welcome here."

The men left us to bleed, to die, and to wail.

After a time the wagon and Mother Evangeline returned to the bloody shop. There was not much of her son left to mourn. "Sister Hannah, I counted on you for protection. Is this the way my son is protected?" she spat at me.

"Voices!" Mother Evangeline glared at me. "I will give you loud voices."

The Patriarch returned, silent for once.

"Ah, our Father," Mother Evangeline said bitingly to him. She threw herself upon him, shaking him fiercely. "Here to protect us until the end of time."

"I will send him where these dogs cannot bite him," is all she said as she buried William that evening. She stayed by the newly dug grave throughout the long night.

The Patriarch was not senior enough to be chosen as a hostage.

The Missourians demanded that first our leaders be surrendered and tried for treason, that we give up our arms, that our property be confiscated, that we all leave the state. The Prophet Joseph prophesied that we would return to Missouri as our rightful home in a generation. Perhaps his timing was off. Who knew when we might return to this vile Eden? I knew the voices told me, but I could not understand.

Brother Brigham led us out of Missouri, another sojourn in our flight to Zion.

JULY 30, 1862
SWEETVILLE

I listen again for the safety of the tongues. I still am the mother of the eldest son, Aaron, for my firstborn Evan has proved unworthy and is cast out. We are surrounded by vile Lamanites. That viper in our midst, Sister Sarah. That abomination to Christ, Twin Spirit, who led Evan astray. That untrustworthy, wounded Chief Sagwitch. It is no wonder that there is murder in our midst. Our enemies are everywhere.

Woe is me. This generation of snakes shall not escape the damnation of hell. In the pollution and abomination of these murders, darkness covers the earth. All flesh is becoming afflicted before my face. Everywhere there are secrets, but I alone must know the truth, for I am given the gift of tongues. If only I could understand their benedictions.

I go into the kitchen to warm some mushrooms. I listen as they cackle out the truth to me. So that is the murderer, I think. Should

CHAPTER TWELVE

I tell or should I hold it close as my secret? I laugh at the humor of it all.

Sister Sarah and Sister Nona join me. The Shoshone speaks, "Do not eat too many mushrooms, Sister Hannah. You will spoil your dinner." Was it me or did I see her smile?

I mutter, "The tongues are so clear today. I understand everything. It all is so obvious."

If this be the Passion, let it come. I am ready.

No one listens. I want to scream but I am voiceless.

CHAPTER THIRTEEN

Brother Eugene

JULY 30, 1862
SWEETVILLE

Brother Port was the one who fetched me. "Another has died."

"Who?"

"Sister Hannah. The third wife."

"How?"

"She had just eaten mushrooms."

I remembered the scene with Evan. How quick Sister Hannah had been to reject her son. What a tumultuous day: to cast aside a first son and then to die from eating mushrooms.

I went to the kitchen with Port.

Sister Sarah and Sister Katherine were there cleaning up Sister Hannah's vomit. The body of Sister Hannah had already been moved to the quiet of the Gold Room.

"Where did the mushrooms come from?" I asked.

"From their allotted space in the cupboard," Sister Sarah answered quietly.

"Who put them there?" I asked.

CHAPTER THIRTEEN

"I am the mushroom picker," she said matter-of-factly.

Sister Katherine defended her. "But who knows what else may have been added in that slot? We all knew that Sister Hannah loved to fry mushrooms as she listened for the tongues. She was the only mushroom eater here."

Who knew that? Every member of this vanishing family.

But I did not have time to be a detective. I must be a scribe.

JULY 31, 1862
SWEETVILLE

For solace I worked on the first part of the preamble through the night. I counted the words. I tightened the rhetoric, adjusting it to a tempo worthy of Isaiah. I filled the allotted pages with an obligatory syntax, a penned-in story, part old and part new, with its own horizon. It sported its own diction and rules. I voiced what others had thought.

I remembered how the Patriarch had rejected his son Evan. He was a Prophet who had not battled for the soul of his son.

That long night I found doubts. Was this true Prophecy or not?

The next morn I asked for an audience with the Patriarch. I told him about my doubts about what I was writing. About its truthfulness and its provenance.

"Be strong, Brother Eugene. When you and I write, we write as one. Together we are full of God's words. Let them come out. Though we should stumble in our placement of words, we shall not fear, lest the Gentiles mock us by their usage. God is our ultimate editor."

I asked the Patriarch, my would-be Father, if this Prophecy was real or counterfeit.

"Our Prophecy is real. It is imminent. You, as my scribe, must submit to the Lord as a child to his Father. You must forget your disobedient ways. Our Church is the true Father and together within it we are Brothers."

I looked away, for once unconvinced.

"Does not this Church cast out its sons?" I asked. "As you have cast out your son Evan?"

"A sinner unrepentant cannot be my son."

"Then can I?"

"Do not be dazzled like a bee at a closed window, forever outside." He continued, "Come inside, Brother Eugene."

"To come inside, so that I gain for you the title of Prophet." I would not be used.

"No, decidedly no. I am a Prophet. Of that you can have no doubt. I have been put on this earth to complete the narrative of the Book of Mormon. I will triumph over the carpenter who lacks the skill of Prophecy. He believes he can split me off. Perhaps he will excommunicate me, but even through that form of death my Prophecy will persevere."

He paused. "But this is about you, Brother Eugene. You are being asked to seed a field that is already plowed. Nothing more, nothing less."

I was stuffed full of the Patriarch's authoritative words. I was tempted by the Patriarch's prophetic assurance. I wanted to be his son. I wanted to remain attracted to this religion in constant flux in this land teeming with would-be Prophets. My desperate, pattern-

CHAPTER THIRTEEN

less self-defense had to diminish. I had to accept this newfound modesty.

I tried to bind myself to this Mormon outside order with its plethora of books to hem me in. I had to wrap myself closely in the mantles of its order, proud of the integrity of its peculiarities. Was not Mormonism, this concocted religion, an amalgamation of all that had gone before, as worthy of belief as any? For that one moment I still believed.

"What is this book I see you reading?" I pointed at the book turned over on the desk.

"*View of the Hebrews* by Ethan Smith. The Prophet found inspiration here. Take it, read it. Everything is open to you, my scribe."

I read some of the book quickly and returned to it later that long evening. I found there words, whole phrases, but mostly I found in *View of the Hebrews* the seminal idea of a lost tribe of Israel coming to America. This tribe had a lost book. They split in two with the triumph of the war-like Lamanites over the back-sliding Nephites.

This was the idea that the Prophet Joseph purloined into his Golden Book. Added imagination. Added a lifetime of reading the Old and the New Testaments in the diction of the King James Bible. Added poetry and fiction, some good, some close to doggerel.

Imagine Joseph Smith wanting to write a historical novel. He finds a source book for some ideas, an outline, a crutch. Then he goes within himself and imagines a story with all its connections. Suppose that once the book takes shape, he forgets how he has used his sources and overrides his plan that it be a novel. Instead it is a revelation, and his writing is a reception of the Word.

Thus the Prophet Joseph used *View of the Hebrews*. It would also explain why the Patriarch might use the same book to concoct his preamble to the Book of Mormon.

Had the Patriarch invented his calling from God? No more than the Prophet Joseph had, or no less. The Patriarch believed he was chosen by God. God had sent him this inspiration, possibly even the source material. He was convinced that his calling was genuine. Though he might manufacture a prelude to the Book of Mormon, in doing so he was convinced that he was doing God's bidding. I trusted that Prophets like the Patriarch did find truth in the strictures of their ongoing, all too human, revelation.

The Prophet and the Patriarch were not plagiarists. They used ideas, phrases, sequences, connections, rethought them, added in their imagination and constructed yet another book. Be it the Book of Mormon or its proposed prequel, Another Book of Mormon, our tale of the Levites. I could not mock their methodology, for was I not also in search of a book built upon the foundation of my research into the Patriarch's family? Books engender books. How well must all authors hide the products that were plundered?

I, a mere scribe, saw ample evidence of the source books of literary device.

Some say that the provenance of a book must be clear and that it is either true or false. I knew better. Every book is equal parts truth and falsity, like all fiction or religion or history. Each cannot totally escape the sham authority that claims revelation, for ultimately there is ever a fiction writer at its source.

Placated, I thought, I scribed onward until I had rid myself of the first part.

CHAPTER THIRTEEN

AUGUST 1, 1862
SWEETVILLE

After completing the first part, I awoke in disbelief, my conversion undone by cold fact and dry criticism. In an instant, querulous of mind, I chose disbelief. I no longer accepted this comforting, badly wanted plaster of a Mormon God. I was unable to yield ownership of myself to this active Mormon God, continuous in his revelation. I could not entrust myself to the belief of the Patriarch.

It was ultimately laughter that decided me to reject the offer from the Patriarch. I laughed at myself as a Prophet's scribe. I, Eugene Lannon, as a Mormon scribbler! A sardonic editor of Prophecy! Even writing for the Herald was not that low.

I was too small to be a Mormon. I accepted the truth of Mormonism for some, though it not be for me. Most of the wives of the Patriarch found some solace in the Mormon way. But I could not receive my belief in God from the imagination of the Patriarch. I did not have the aptitude for such an unquestioning belief. I could not trust this Mormon God to enforce my world into a firm balance. I was too sarcastic to surrender my volition without doubt. I must soldier on alone, an unsaved remnant, fatherless, a sickly soul without solace, facing a silent heaven. I must make do with knowing my dry, divided, homeless self.

I remembered what Twin Spirit had told Evan. Choose that which makes you yourself. By choosing you will find your way. I remembered Whitman's need for adhesiveness between manly spirits and the rich, sexual duality of Twin Spirit, the ma ai'pots. Yes, for me, Twin Spirit was more of a true prophet than the Patriarch. I heard something from him that heralded what only I must become.

My sexual life was in turmoil. I could no longer bed Abigail, and she had fled to a more reliable and bountiful source, Abel. She prepared to leave with him, engorged with his Western-themed, marketable sketches. My marriage, a dwarfed pear with a worm at its core, was over. In honesty I admitted to myself that I was well quit of her. Would I ever know desire again? What had the ritual dance of the ma ai'pots taught me? What did desire look like? I could not imagine.

I needed to reclaim the shell of my own words, my own thoughts, my own halting detection. My voice was no longer dead. It had been tested by the Patriarch's tight system, but somehow my own voice had survived. I was at liberty. I was a child of disobedience. I was a singular author with my own tales to tell. I could make of the Patriarch's family a story. I could find the testimony of each of the Sisters. Who cared whether I dub it fiction or not?

I was a detective, not a scribe. I may in the future pretend to be a scribe, but rightly I was a detective. I gave up the comfort of editing Prophecy. Though I would not tell the Patriarch that yet. Perhaps Prophecy was somehow at the root of these murders.

I must finish this investigation, focus on this sprawl of murders.

Sisters seven, five, and three were murdered. Mother Evangeline, wife one, slept alone in the Gold Room. How might I protect her?

I had listened to so much about each wife. I had to continue to attend to the stories of the wives in this shrinking family but seemed

CHAPTER THIRTEEN

unable to imagine connections that explained this mystery. I wrote and thought in a jumble of the past and present tenses. I researched and imagined their flashbacks, but I could not understand the arc of the story. I did not take hashish, hitherto my trusty tool, as an aid to my insight. I had to find the key myself.

Doctor Peter and Brother Brigham's spy, Brother Port, were the only ones besides myself who seemed to care about our dilemma. But their motivations, grief, and pinning faults on the Patriarch were not conducive to adept investigation. The Patriarch himself was caught up in the completion of his Prophecy. Murder for him was a petty, personal annoyance.

I failed as I tried to think of suspects or motivation.

Sister Sarah? Yes, she might be said to hate the Gold Room wives more for the threat of constraint by birthing males that they embody than for anything they did to her. As a Shoshone, she had much need of punishing Mormons. She was adept at poisons. She gathered them and mushrooms and brewed tea. Sister Hannah had hated the perfidy that Twin Spirit brought to her son, Evan, but that hardly seemed motivation for Sister Sarah to murder her.

Twin Spirit? He lacked motivation. He was no more a suspect than the Patriarch himself. Both Prophets did not make compelling murderers. They were too obsessed with Prophecy to concoct mayhem.

Sister Nona? She hated the Patriarch and loathed the Sisterdom.

Sister Willa? Her own would-be son may have been a victim. She was certainly organized enough to plot and execute these murders, but when has sheer industry been an ample motivation?

Sister Katherine? I had yet to research her past, to fashion her flashback. She was too saintly for murder. But saints, betrayed, may be murderers.

Mother Evangeline? As the first wife, the last inhabitant of the Gold Room, she seemed slated more for victim than perpetrator. I had gleaned some of her past from the other Sisters. I had to watch her more closely.

CHAPTER FOURTEEN

The Testimony of Sister Katherine, the Second Wife

AUGUST 1, 1862

SWEETVILLE

I, who gladly faces my own death, sing for each of the murdered Sisters. When I sing, my voice opens to God, I am comforted. When I begin again, sing another verse, I know that I sing truthfully and comfort others.

Everything that happens is brightened by our Sisterdom in the Blue Room in this house rent by murders. What may be taking place may seem meaningless, tortured, and sad, but I believe in the simplicity of God's silence. He will make everything clear. In all modesty, I am awake to God's immanent luminosity. He belongs to me. I believe in the essential goodness of this, His given life. I give Him my joyous consent in supreme trust. I await calmly His Word, assured that He will make known those who threaten us.

The heaven within me is more benign than any elevation that the Patriarch might promise by the birth of a son. I thank God that I have birthed only two fine daughters, for I accept but do not covet the Gold Room. I do not question God for having joined my lot with the Patriarch. I stand face-to-face with God, bounded in recognition, alone, needing no Celestial bindings, conscious of His presence without a need to see Him, ever born anew in His spirit.

Meanwhile I pour the assurance of my salvation into my Sisterdom. Such sweet bindings, not Celestial, but still of a fine, eternal sheen. Despite my approaching death, a death that will neither come too soon nor be too distant, I trust in the jewel-like spirit as it daily renews my bodily strength from the threats of my ever-present consumption. My inner harp's ecstatic music cries out to my Sisters, particularly Sister Sarah, in the unsure days of her motherhood. I sing each day with a certitude that demands no conductor's baton.

I turn to Sister Sarah, awakening, spooned by my side, "Last night was the sweetest night I ever had in my life. I never before, for so long a time together, enjoyed so much of the light and rest and sweetness of heaven in my soul. I relaxed as if the cooling waters of a stream flowed over me. I felt not the least agitation of body during the whole time. I felt God's favor. It is not mine to will anything, but to will nothing. I am resigned to whatever death God wills me. I shall easily endure whatever pain God wills upon me."

"But what of me, Sister Katherine?" Sister Sarah stirs. "If you are gone, how can I go on without you? I lack your faith in the Mormon God and the Mormon way."

"We accept each other totally and find strength in our Sisterdom. Look to the others, Sister Willa, Sister Nona."

"Sister Willa will help. Sister Nona hates me. She offers nothing. I know they will not be enough. Without you, the Blue Room will seem empty. I can only stomach this Mormon life with you,

CHAPTER FOURTEEN

who are so stately and womanly. I only can be a Mormon within the safety of this Blue Room. With you. Under your protection. You make it acceptable. The melody and measure of your speech is like a refrain to a blessed hymn. If I were to lose you, I would rather live alone, or perhaps return to my people, the Shoshone, if they would acknowledge me. There I could live out my time, if these Mormons would only allow it."

"What of the Patriarch?"

"He is nothing to me. I shall never forgive him."

"He does not need your forgiveness. Accept, and you shall be accepted. Find safety in the delightful conviction of that wonderful truth."

"Could I ever forgive those who have tormented my people?" Sister Sarah spits out. "It was not the Mormons who were the murderers, but they called the army to this Valley, so they are also guilty. Why should I forgive my Mormon husband, this Patriarch? Was he not but the clamor that brought forth the murderers? How should he be punished? And when?"

"You will find faith in the gentle touch of time and responsibility, and that will make everything necessary and easy. It is no trifling thing to be a Saint. It takes an arduous toiling. We must plant shade trees along the canals so that the Angels come and instruct us in the line of our duties, as they would not come if there was no shade for them to rest under. Plant and cultivate your trees, Sister Sarah. Therein you will find your own answer in Motherhood and Sisterdom. That will suffice."

"Will it? Must it? I am not assured."

"You must accept your sacrifice without complaint. I did."

JANUARY 15, 1837
KIRTLAND, OHIO

I sat alone, quietly awaiting the final argument. The light was fading on this wintry day. There was not much time left me.

Both the Prophet and Brother Sweet—later called the Patriarch—came into the parlor, cornering me. The Prophet dressed persuasively for the occasion in a blue dress coat and pants, a black, silk, and velvet vest, white cravat, and a black cane. Brother Sweet dressed all in black. He did not try to sway me by his plenitude.

"Sister Katherine," Brother Sweet spoke first, "I am required by the Lord to take another wife. The Lord has given you to me as one of my spiritual wives. I have the blessings of Jacob granted me, as he granted holy men of old, and I have looked upon you with favor, and I hope you will not deny me. I have no flattering words to offer. It is the command of God."

"Have you not already a wife? Is not Sister Evangeline sufficient?"

"No, the Lord has seen fit to reward me for my travails. I am plenteous and must multiply."

I turned to the Prophet. "We Mormons were not always polygamous. Why now?"

"Our first view of marriage was given when our Church was in its infancy, when we were babes, and had to be fed on milk, but now we are strong and we must have meat. We must practice the marriage ways of Solomon and David."

I felt uncertainty. "Prophet, I would rather you teach this revelation to someone else."

CHAPTER FOURTEEN

"Sister Katherine, it is your duty as a woman of searching heart to accept, for such preach the Lord through my revelation. You are the singer whose voice leads others. Give voice to my revelation." The Prophet took my hand forcefully and gave it to my suitor. "You must accept Brother Sweet."

"But will my song be heard amongst so many?" I asked the Prophet.

"The Lord will hear and He will make sure that you are heard by others. Your voice, your ornament, will not be wasted."

My eyes looked to my suitor.

"Brother Sweet, how should I know if you are doing this to honor God or to dishonor and debauch me? How shall I tell the difference?"

The Prophet Joseph grew short. "To live in plurality is part of the restitution of all things. In ancient times under the law of God, the permission of a plurality of wives prevented the possibility of fornication in the wife. You must accept plurality in order to retain purity."

"But what if I should feel dirty? How can I face Sister Evangeline? Will she not look at me as one wanton?"

"My first wife shall be like a Mother to you," Brother Sweet reasoned. "You that are an orphan shall find family."

"You have her approval?"

"I have not sought her consent. The Prophet has decreed plurality. I have found you."

The Prophet spoke, "If any man espouse a virgin, and desire to espouse another, let the first give her consent. And if he espouse the second, and they are virgins, and have vowed to no other man, then he is justified. He cannot commit adultery, for they are given unto him, for he cannot commit adultery with that that belongeth unto them, and to none else. And if he have ten virgins given onto him by law, he cannot commit adultery, for they belong to him, and they are given unto him. Therefore he is justified."

The Prophet talked of consent of the first wife, a consent Brother Sweet did not deem necessary.

Brother Sweet threatened me, "If you not obey the command of God concerning plural marriage, you will be damned."

The Prophet was at first harsh. "It is the command of God to you to wed Brother Sweet. Accept, and you will gain eternal salvation. If you reject His message, the gate will be closed forever to you."

I shuddered.

The Prophet Joseph smiled at me with his light blue eyes. "Whenever I see a pretty woman, I have to pray for grace. Brother Sweet is most fortunate. It is your combined lot to multiply and strengthen Zion. Sister Katherine, submit yourself to your husband, Brother Sweet."

I believed in the Prophet. I took what he said straight from the fountain.

The room darkened as the sun set. My soul was filled with a calm, sweet peace that I had not previously known. Supreme happiness took possession of me for a brief moment. I felt that I had received a powerful and irresistible testimony of the truth of plural marriage. I felt that I now had an anchor for the trials of life.

"Have you decided, Sister Katherine?" the Prophet asked.

I nodded and the two rose to leave me.

Just then Sister Evangeline entered to light the lamp.

CHAPTER FOURTEEN

The Prophet turned to her. "Sister Evangeline, you must receive Sister Katherine as the handmaiden onto Brother Sweet for so I have decided."

Sister Evangeline looked hard at Brother Sweet. She would not look my way. She had not agreed to this plurality. She confronted Brother Sweet, "Whoring spirit!" She left the room.

AUGUST 1, 1862
SWEETVILLE

I happen upon Brother Eugene, who looks tired from too long a night. He looks at me concerned. I lead him to the music room and sit down to play a simple hymn. I sing to buoy up him whose faith wavers. I sing softly but still am short of breath. I stop my song.

"You do not look well, Sister Katherine. Sit for a moment with me and rest." We are silent together. I have already told him my tale.

"Do not worry about your faltering faith, Brother Eugene. If it is God's will, you will believe. If it is not, you will not."

"Am I that transparent?" he asks softly.

"No, you hide yourself well. But as my time approaches, I see clearly and voice what I see directly. When it is time, God through his grace will show you the way."

"Is that way the Church of the Latter Day Saints?"

"Who knows, time will tell."

"If not, what will be the outcome of my life?"

"Who knows? You are a seeker, a detective of life. Seek."

"But is that enough?"

"It must be enough for it is what you are."

"And what of my detection? Can God help me there?"

"No, for these murders are the work of the Devil. You must solve them yourself."

"But how?"

"The world is a benign place. God in His infinite wisdom does not construct problems that we, mere mortals, cannot solve."

"But what if there not be enough clues?"

"The past and the present are full of clues. Listen to what is said and what is not said. Focus your whole heart and mind on the truth and you will find the only answer."

"You give me hope, Sister Katherine, thank you. I go back to my Mormon mystery renewed."

CHAPTER FIFTEEN

✂—

Eugene Lannon (No Longer Brother Eugene)

AUGUST 2, 1862
SWEETVILLE

Abigail and I strolled outside through Sweetville's fecund fields.

"Eugene, or should I call you Brother Eugene?" Abigail laughed at me.

"Call me what you like," I said without any anger in my voice.

"Eugene, then." She paused. "You know our time together, this so-called marriage is over."

"Of course it is over. I no longer satisfy you."

"We no longer satisfy each other. It has just taken this open space amongst the Mormons in this strange place to acknowledge it."

"You have looked around and seen other alternatives. What will it be? A Mormon Prophet?"

"Wouldn't that be a lark! No, I don't see myself as a populace for the emptying Gold Room or the still full Blue."

"I'm sure you could negotiate your own room or even your own house here. The Patriarch is quite ready to spawn sons upon you."

"Could you just see me as a Mormon, me a mother, in this Godforsaken place!" Abigail laughed and I remembered briefly the charming flirt I had married.

"Yes, even you would not do something so risible. Regardless of the ample fruits that might await you."

"I shall wed Abel," she said with assurance.

"Ah, the ever-ample Abel. May you grace his commodious salon with its overstuffed landscapes."

"You are right. He is not a great painter. But he is popular and has other attractions."

"Spare me the catalog." I stopped her short. "When?"

"Soon. After we two are divorced."

"And how is this to happen, this divorce?"

"That is easy, now that you are playing the Mormon. We will ask the Patriarch to dissolve our marriage."

"Yes, the randy Patriarch will do that for sure. He will think you have signed on as a future Sister."

"Just like he thinks you have converted to be his scribe."

"What if I have truly converted?" I asked, trying to add doubt to my voice.

"Eugene, come now, this is Abigail you are speaking to. Not some would-be Prophet. You are no more a Mormon scribe than I am a Sister-in-waiting."

We both laughed together at the comic turn of our connubial play.

"We will go to the Patriarch this afternoon and dissolve this drollery."

We parted without choler. As she walked away, she did not turn

CHAPTER FIFTEEN

to look back. I continued on down the path towards the river.

I came upon Sister Sarah and Twin Spirit talking.

"What will you do next?" Twin Spirit asked his sister.

"I will wait until all of this is over. Then I will leave this place."

"If they let you. Where will you go?"

"I will go wherever I will be accepted." She saw me then and, perhaps thinking me a spy, panicked. She fled toward the village.

Twin Spirit joined me quietly. He, Evan-less, looked as lost as I felt.

"Wandering. Deep, deep in thought," he read me.

"Pondering change. Not knowing what be next," I mused.

"Change is all around. Death and life. Everywhere change."

"How will I know what is the right path?"

"Just travel. The path will become clear."

"What will happen? To me, to this family, to the Shoshone?"

"The Great Spirit will show us all in time."

"But what about now?" I demanded.

"This is what I see. I see you deepening. That is the goal in your life now, this deepening."

"But what about the fear of the future?"

"What is there to dread? Do not worry. Accept life in its endless variation."

Twin Spirit left me alone. I had a marriage to end and a murderer to find.

AUGUST 2, 1862
SWEETVILLE

Abigail took the lead in the play before the Patriarch. I assumed a meek silence.

"Brother Eugene and I have come before you, worthy Patriarch, to entreat your aid."

"What is it, Abigail?" the Patriarch asked pointedly.

"Our marriage has floundered. It is barren. We no longer have congress."

"Of course you do not entwine. You are not fated for each other. You, Abigail, have been spiritually bound to another. Your body has not found its true husband. Brother Eugene has other tasks to complete. He has found his calling as my scribe."

"What is the right solution, Patriarch?" Abigail asked in the cloak of modesty.

"When a marriage is over, is irreconcilable, a Bishop in the territory of Utah can dissolve it."

"Brother Eugene?" the Patriarch asked sternly.

"Yes, Prophet."

"Is this marriage a fiction?"

"Yes, it is no more."

"Fairest Abigail?"

"Yes, Patriarch."

"Is it your desire to rid yourself of this encumbrance and find a new spiritual path?"

"Truly, Patriarch. I wish to find the correct spiritual husband."

"Bow your heads, my children. Then in the power vested in me in the Mormon Church and the Utah territory, I dissolve this marriage effective immediately."

Abigail's smile was almost a smirk. She held herself back from

CHAPTER FIFTEEN

laughing out loud, but just barely.

The Patriarch seemed to wait for some solemnity to settle in before he might ask a follow-up question. But the solemn moment never came. Abigail shot the Patriarch and myself another triumphant smile and left us alone in the Patriarch's study.

It took the Patriarch a few moments to digest what had just happened. He was pensive, almost unsure.

But the ways of Prophecy came back to the fore.

"How do you progress, scribe?" the Patriarch asked.

"I have finished the first half of the preamble. I have edited it, smoothed it out, worked at making its diction consistent with the Book. Here it is." I thrust it down on the desk. "What is next? When shall I see the second section?"

"I am still receiving the Prophecy. I have more tablets to decipher. It is not ready for you yet."

"When, Prophet, when?" I asked, feigning the scribe.

"Soon, scribe, soon."

He sent me away empty-handed.

I passed an agitated Mother Evangeline as I exited the study. "I trust your writing goes well, Brother Eugene?" she said with an edge to her voice

As the door closed, I heard her ask loudly, "Where is it? What have you done with it?"

"I am not done with it yet. I must complete the second part," the Patriarch answered. She, the first wife, must be privy to the evolving Prophecy.

As I walked slowly to my soon solitary cabin, I spent little time wondering at the speed at which I became single. I had lost Abigail long before to the more bountiful Abel and did not regret it.

At last I rejected the Prophet's empty immanence, this so-called missing link. I was not sure how he did it, but I knew his revelations, with its divine pretense of Prophecy, was a sham. He was a cribber, or an author, but he was no Prophet. Was his so-called preamble, another Book, a blatant forgery from some other source or a work of an all too human authorship confused by a divine spark?

I pondered how the original Book of Mormon contained many similarities to Ethan Smith's *View of the Hebrews*, that book I had borrowed from the Patriarch's desk. Surely this earlier book, while perhaps a source for Joseph Smith, his scribes, and perhaps now for the Patriarch, was not a sufficient explanation for the first Book or its proposed prequel. The earlier work presented itself as history, not an elaborated, American, thousand-year Gospel. In it a Jewish tribe came to America and this "stick of Joseph and Ephraim" engendered the savage tribes of American Indians. There were the inevitable echoes of the Prophet Isaiah. There were even sacred records buried in a hill. But there was just not enough in Ethan Smith to explain the Book of Mormon, let alone the nascent Another Book. Ethan Smith may have been read, but he was not the principle source. Something else explained Joseph Smith's Book and the Patriarch's.

Before I went to sleep that night, I stopped worrying about Prophecy and tried to re-focus on the murders. I revisited all I had learned about the Prophet, his wives, their stories. I had spied and eavesdropped and asked questions, but it was all so disjunctive. I felt like a crank who could not piece things together. All of the murdered wives were sealed, Gold Room-housed, and odd-numbered wives.

CHAPTER FIFTEEN

Only one odd-numbered wife remained, Mother Evangeline. She knew about the Prophecy. She had to be the next to be threatened. I had to protect her. I couldn't let her imbibe anything!

CHAPTER SIXTEEN

✂

The Testimony of Mother Evangeline, the First Wife

AUGUST 4, 1862
SWEETVILLE

"I do not want or need your protection, Brother Eugene," I answer the prying journalist.

"But you are at risk, Mother Evangeline."

"With the Lord's full support, I need no other."

"You are the last sealed wife. You are alone in the Gold Room."

"I am not afraid of being solitary, Brother." I give him a title he does not deserve. "After all these years with my fellow Sisters, it is almost a blessing."

"Who is doing this? Who is trying to destroy the family?"

"How should I know? I don't pose as a detective. That is your charge to discover."

"How is the Patriarch reacting to these murders, Mother?"

"He barely notices them. All those who have died have been sealed, so their fate is decided. He has a Prophet's work to perform. What heed need he pay to mere mortality?"

"Prophecy comes slowly," the spying scribe says.

CHAPTER SIXTEEN

"Particularly for those who witness its source," I say, waving him away.

Finally my gesture drives this detective from my midst.

I am the 'Cyria Electa', the first of the wives, as the Patriarch calls me. All of his subsequent wives are mere afterthoughts, Sisters for the Patriarch to dally upon. Some be sealed, some not. I am the Mother of this family, but remain cold to these other Sisters. I do not caress or kiss like those saintly, loving women of the Blue Room. Blessedly, I am finally alone in the quiet Gold Room.

I remain in contact with Emma Smith, the true Prophet's first wife. She does not believe in this polygamy, this abomination, this Sisterdom, nor do her followers. It may have been simpler to go with her, to follow her in exile from Brother Brigham's sect, but my fate is here with the Patriarch. I must bear witness to his Prophecy, even if he failed to give witness to another's.

I have lost my unprotected son. It was decreed that I would have one living son and be rightly sealed. After that one son was no more, I have been left barren. The Patriarch does not call me to his bed. He spills his errant seed elsewhere. Good riddance.

I believe in the divisions of the afterlife. There are indeed three heavens and one hell. Each are separated chapters in the master tome. Sisters Karita and Hannah are in the Celestial Heaven awaiting the Patriarch. Sister Prudence is there at the side of the true Prophet Joseph.

JUNE 8, 1830
PALMYRA, NEW YORK

The Prophet Joseph was like a calf who suckled on many udders. He devoured books, whatever his new scribe, Oliver Cowdery, had him read, like *View of the Hebrews*. He read and re-read the Old and the New Testament. He emptied his editor's udders. He turned Cowdery, a failed teacher, into the ultimate scribe. He nursed on the stories that his wild dreams told. There can be no true Prophecy without a touch of madness. For it is only the mad who God converts into a true Prophet.

"I am a channel through which God needs pass," he said. "I am wholly His instrument. My own mind is naught. I am immortal, not the mortal body of Joseph you see before you. I have been chosen not for my learning, but because the Lord prefers the weak things of the world, those who are unlearned and mocked, to bring the word of the nations. The Lord hath delivered this Book to me who is not of the learned. He hath given me the strength to finish its translation."

We believed him when he said that he, dressed in black, riding a black horse with a switch tail, had found these plates on this hill of dry bones where the Nephites were defeated by the savage Lamanites. He sang to us a song of future and former times. He juggled fiction and religion, forever masking their boundaries. And from him our new religion, this fresh, lucrative spring, was born.

Martin Harris, my foolish brother with his flighty wife, had tried to be the Prophet's first scribe. His feeble attempts, those errant one hundred sixteen pages, were garbled, unedited, the work of a dumbly recording secretary. Lucy Harris was a rank infidel, unworthy even of such a fool as my brother. She fought hard the attention, financial and otherwise, that Martin gave to recording this true Prophecy. She seized this dictation and tried to hide it

CHAPTER SIXTEEN

away, but I found it feebly hidden under the coverlet and protected it. It was too early, a first attempt. The pages lacked the sparkling sweep of Prophecy. Thankfully Lucy Harris, my disbelieving sister-in-law, had purloined them. After I stole them from her bedroom, I read them in horror and hid them away for a later time.

The Prophet Joseph started again recognizing he needed a worthier scribe. He did not redo the missing pages despite the taunts of the shrew, Lucy Harris, for Prophecy, once transcribed, cannot be repeated. He said the missing pages were held in reserve by the Devil, that should anyone attempt to retranslate them, the Devil would bring forth the original. But I was not of the Devil, or perhaps I was as I spirited them away.

My brother, Martin, was an unworthy scribe. So the Prophet Joseph followed the Lord's direction and found his fitting, correcting, transcribing, smoothing editor. Oliver Cowdery, his dark hair growing comically in tufts behind his ears, was divinely commanded. He was sent by the Lord to record. These days were never to be forgotten by those who were there. The Prophet's voice, liquored up for the mighty task of translation, could be heard intoning page by page, verse by verse, day by day. The inspiration of heaven called with its sudden stroke of ideas. Joseph would pause, read once more the Bible, become again a humble Prophet, and then new revelation would come direct from his mouth. Cowdery edited it, tried to make it more coherent, for the Prophet Joseph spoke with an imperfect voice. Who knew where Prophecy ended and editing began? Some of it seemed quite familiar as it echoed from the Bible, other parts were wildly new. Their tempo accelerated. Six hundred fresh pages came in a mere seventy-five days.

How could this revelation have happened? Who could keep track of the hundreds of characters and place names? Who could master this timeline? Who could concoct a story with so many voices? Was it from God or were other men, informed, creative men, making it all up?

The Prophet said there were plates under the blanket, but what need was there for plates to translate from when their Prophecy was so clear? Who could find fraud in this clear a revelation?

Then, the chosen were asked to bear witness.

Three were asked to swear that they beheld and saw the plates. Cowdery as scribe was first. "I have had seasons of skepticism, but I believe in this Golden Bible. I believe it comes from God and should be witnessed. We were divinely commanded." How could an editor, the ultimate insider, question the righteousness of an author?

Harris, my scatterbrained brother, who had lost the missing pages, signed next. "I have seen the plates with the eye of faith."

Whitmer, the third witness, tried to smooth down his hair, which flew heavenward. "I not only saw the Book of Mormon. I saw other plates, other books," he attested to the abundant continuity of revelation.

All three of these witnesses, their work done, later left the Church and became enemies of the Prophet.

Like the Twelve Apostles and the twelve tribes, the Prophet asked for a total of Twelve Witnesses. Nine more were needed. Perhaps he used the testimony of the lead three witnesses as a lever to induce nine more to sign an instrument even though some hesitated. They were asked to swear that they had handled the unseen plates, that they had felt their heft. They were asked to give evidence

CHAPTER SIXTEEN

of things weighed but not seen.

The Prophet Joseph commanded, "Your testimonies shall rise up to condemn the unbelieving and rebellious before the judgment seat of Christ. You need not look into the box that contains the plates, for that is holy. You need only attest that the plates exist and that the book is indeed a translation of them."

Eight signed.

"But what if the box does not contain plates?" my would-be husband, John Sweet, declaimed. "I have been shown a box and felt its fifty-pound weight. For all I know the box may contain only rocks."

"O ye of little faith!" the Prophet bellowed. "How long will God bear with this wicked and perverse generation? Down on your knees. Come forward, John Sweet, and be a part of this great awakening."

John Sweet fell to the floor.

My brother sneered, "What if it is a lie? If you follow us, you will make money out of it. Now is the time for a new religion to arise."

"I have seen you, Joseph Smith," John Sweet arose, "sit by a table and put a handkerchief to your forehead and peek into your hat and call out a word to Cowdery, who sits at the same table and writes something down. That is all I can attest to."

"But there must be Twelve who swear to the truth of the plates. Twelve is the number I need."

"Some revelations are of God. Some revelations are of men. And some revelations are of the Devil. How can I know what yours are? Show me the plates. Now."

"I no longer have them. They have been taken from me. God has ordered me to re-bury them," he answered breathlessly. "They are hidden for safekeeping. They will reappear when they are needed."

"How convenient, Prophet," John Sweet shouted. "Then I cannot be a part of this scheme of the Golden Bible. Find another witness."

"John Sweet, let us wrestle for it. If I win, you bear witness."

"No, Joseph Smith. Again I say no."

"I will witness for you," I raised my voice. "I will replace my disbelieving betrothed."

"Sister," the Prophet said softly, "I cannot accept a woman's belief, though you be the softest of witnesses. It is your betrothed or no one. John Sweet, you have seen and hefted the box of plates. Attest to it!"

John Sweet grabbed the manuscript and added to the Testimony of the Witnesses, "John Sweet certifies that he believes it not." He signed it with a flourish.

AUGUST 4, 1862
SWEETVILLE

The would-be scribbler is here again, that fool who the Patriarch courts as his Cowdery. Brother Eugene intercepts me as I come from the sacred study.

I shake his ministrations off as Sister Sarah approaches.

"Brew me some Mormon tea," I order her.

She does as her Mother rightfully bids her. It takes a few minutes. The Patriarch joins us. We keep him from his Prophecy.

The scribbler faces me, watching.

"So this is the drink you brew for me!" I exclaim. "Shall I drink it

CHAPTER SIXTEEN

and be beaten down as you have murdered Sisters Karita, Prudence, and Hannah, you Shoshone slut!"

Sister Sarah does not appear riled.

"Let us feed it to the dog," the Patriarch says, "to test its contents."

Brother Eugene looks on.

"I will drink it first," Sister Sarah says. "Why risk a dog!"

"Yes, certainly when a Shoshone will do," I spit forth.

Sister Sarah retrieves the drink.

"No need, Sister Sarah. No other creature need die." The bogus Brother Eugene stays her hand. "I have heard enough and seen enough. And smelled enough."

He addresses the Patriarch, "John Sweet, call all your wives together. It is time for this deadly masquerade to cease."

"Ask Chief Sagwitch to join us, and Twin Spirit, and Brother Port, even the profligate, Evan, if he has not left. For all must hear this story," he continues.

"But what of your ex-wife, Abigail, and the painter Abel?" the Patriarch asks.

"They have left Utah today, but I guess in some certain way my ex-wife is part of the story. I will tell her if ever I should see her again. She will appreciate the humor."

The Patriarch leaves to gather the audience.

CHAPTER SEVENTEEN

Eugene Lannon

AUGUST 3, 1862
SWEETVILLE

It was as a detective and not a scribe that I faced the dwindled wives of John Sweet. The survivors of the Blue Room, Sisters Sarah, Willa, Nona, and Katherine, huddled together on the sofa. The Patriarch chose a straight-backed chair on the other side of the room. Mother Evangeline chose another straight-backed chair next to him. Brother Port looked on from the right as Brother Brigham's official representative. Chief Sagwitch, Twin Spirit, and Evan all stood to the left. I faced them all.

"I must apologize," I began slowly, "for taking so long to unravel this mystery. I was too busy playing the scribe seduced by Prophecy. The full and particular facts, be they broken and circumstantial, were always there. I just could not focus on them."

I paused. "Numbers. This tale is awash in numbers. The eight wives. The killing by poisoning of the odd-numbered wives. The Gold Room emptied of first the seventh, then the fifth, and lastly the third. All sealed, all bound for the Celestial Kingdom. The threat

CHAPTER SEVENTEEN

to the remaining sealed first wife. The safety of the Blue Room for the even-numbered wives."

"The murders of the three wives were all by poison," I said. "In tea, in pills, by mushrooms. Who found the poison? Probably Sister Sarah. Who placed the poison in the cupboard? Again, probably Sister Sarah. Who added the poison to the two tea containers or a pill jar where it did not belong? That is not as clear. Who then brewed the tea? Sister Sarah. Who brought the pill to Sister Prudence? Sister Nona. Who picked the mushrooms? Perhaps Sister Sarah. Sister Nona knows plants. But it is not the brewer or the bringer or the picker who murdered. The murderer is the one who placed the poison where it did not belong."

I digressed to a silent room, "I was thrown off by the Shoshone angle. The Indian wife, Sister Sarah, the gatherer and dispenser of poisons. Surely she had motive to hate the Patriarch and his sealed wives. Perhaps another Shoshone, the Chief, even Twin Spirit, might have helped her in this plot. Brother Port, that is the solution you offered up. But the Shoshone are not the villains of this story. Twin Spirit is a healer, a seeker, a dispenser of truth. Not a murderer. And Sister Sarah, despite the righteousness of her anger, is not a murderer either."

Sister Sarah, or White Cloud, her rightful name, sat up. Sister Katherine put her arm around the Shoshone maiden in support.

"I tried to imagine Sister Nona as a murderess. She hated the Patriarch and found nothing in her Sisters."

"Numbers," I continued. "Twelve. The Patriarch wanted to be selected as an Apostle. Brother Brigham has sent Port to keep an eye on this would-be Apostle who promises further Prophecy. I was asked to aid this Prophecy, to edit, to scribe, perhaps to witness." At this last word, the Patriarch started and stared straight ahead.

"Yes, to witness, like the Book of Mormon, Another Book must have witnesses. The original Book has three primary witnesses, and eight in concurrence, eleven in total. But what an odd number eleven is. Like the Apostles or the tribes, is not twelve the required number? Shouldn't there be nine concurring witnesses? Twelve in total. What had become of the twelfth witness?"

"I remembered something Brother Brigham had said when arguing with the Patriarch." I fixed my attention on the Patriarch. "Brother Brigham claimed that since you could not witness, you were unworthy of joining the Twelve Apostles."

Mother Evangeline smiled.

"The ninth who would not concur. Wasn't that you, John Sweet?" I raised my voice and shouted out my question. Mother Evangeline nodded in approval. Sister Nona, the ninth daughter, smiled.

"Why could you not be the ninth witness, John Sweet?" I questioned warmly.

"In those times, I took stories too literally. I had not seen the Golden Plates or correctly weighed their presence, so how could I attest to their legitimacy? I was younger then and did not understand the Lord gives truth in odd ways. I have since learned that maintaining a mystery is critical to being accepted. I did not understand that regardless of their provenance books are given to Prophets by God to be sold to sinners." He looked away.

"Nine." I continued. "Eight. The talk of nine. Where had there been the talk of nine?"

CHAPTER SEVENTEEN

"My dearly departed Abigail, no longer my wife, could not remain for our denouement," I said bitterly. "She and Abel are fleeing East, divorce in hand, with a trunk full of marketable Western sketches. Little did she know that she played her part in our plot."

Many of the others, but not all, looked on confused.

"Nine. The Patriarch offered Abigail a spot as his ninth wife. He did not specify the Blue Room or the Gold Room, only time, procreation, and eventual sealing would decide that. Certainly Abigail, if she had been interested, would have driven a hard bargain." The Patriarch's anger grew close to explosion.

"It was the talk of the ninth wife that caused it all. Our murderer, crowded by all those who were sealed and unworthy, could not accept another. He, who would not be the ninth witness, could not have nine wives."

At first I turned to Sister Nona, whose name meant nine, who hated this crowd of Sisterdom. "Was it Sister Nona?"

I paused. "No."

But then I faced the murderess: "Am I right, Mother Evangeline?"

"Yes, the threat of nine wives was the breaking point. Another whore for this brothel. Your wanton wife sniffing around because your salt had lost its savor!" she taunted me.

She turned her chair to face the Patriarch.

"I had accepted much evil, but this was too much to ask of me." She paused. "After all my sacrifice and loss you treated me like a dog. You paraded your bitches before my eyes, and asked me to sleep with them, without privacy. You could not be the ninth witness, but you asked—no, told—me to accept a ninth wife."

The silence in the room was profound.

"As each wife came, I suffered the torments of the damned. Here was my husband, gray-headed, taking to your bed young girls, wanton wives, in a mockery of marriage. Indian squaws, New York Gentile whores. Who would you hanker for next? I loathe this unclean thing you have made, John Sweet, with all the strength of my nature. I could not have it happen again. I had to act."

"I thought you accepted the need for polygamy," the Patriarch said quietly.

"I never consented, you greedy dog, who could never have enough. Not once. You thought I could forget; but I, with this serpent of remembrance within me, never could."

"If the wife can show no good reason why she refuses to comply with the law, which was given to Sarah of old, that it is lawful for her husband, if permitted by the revelation through the Prophet, to be married to others without her consent. By this I am justified," the Patriarch chanted as Mother Evangeline shook her head.

"I have ever withheld my consent, but you went on with it anyway. My consent meant nothing to you. You promised me that each new wife would make no difference in our ties together, that our tie would remain pure and single. It has never been so and never could be so. Polygamy for me has been an abomination of desolation and corruption. Before such form of evil, I could only feign submission."

Sister Katherine wept.

"You said that I would remain the Mother. You would cleave to me that am son less. Yes, I became a bitter Mother, whose son you and that whore Hannah could not protect!"

CHAPTER SEVENTEEN

"I placed you first," the Patriarch muttered. "You were of the Gold Room."

"You promised me a Gold Room. I got a room painted in a color as false as the promises you have made me."

Sister Nona withdrew into herself. Sister Sarah sat up proudly. Sister Willa remained calm.

All looked to the Patriarch.

"Evangeline," he grew cold, "then why did you not divorce me, if you hated me so much?"

"I stayed out of amazement, a desire to watch your perfidy up-close and report back."

"Report back to whom?"

"To God or to the Devil. I did not care which."

"Why not kill the Patriarch himself?" I asked.

"If I must risk my soul, it was more proper that I taunt him with these murders."

"Why kill only the sealed wives?" I further questioned.

"I have only killed those who have accepted without reservation the evil practices that he preaches: self-satisfied Karita, verbose Prudence, un-nurturing Hannah. May they find their proper place in Celestial Heaven!" she spat out her words. "I have weeded out your Celestial wives, John Sweet. I murdered only those who were headed to a Celestial Heaven so that they have time alone there to accept their cursed, blessed fate. May they and you be fit company!"

"How could you murder and as a Mormon not confess your actions?" the Patriarch asked lamely.

"I could not confess my murderer's sins to my Bishop, for it is you, you self-proclaimed Patriarch, you un-bless-worthy Bishop, who is the cause of these murders. I murdered that I stand spot-filled against ye, John Sweet, on the final day. I pondered eternity with you and could not but act in rebellion. The thought of being bound to you for infinite duration in a spiritual prison was too much. You are a vainglorious fraud who could not witness, who could not testify. Yet you accepted the succor of Celestial Marriage, bedding down with more and more, each as they came. I chose an evil which hast its foundation as the arm of God. I chose to welter in the vengeance of eternal fire, so that I might stand blessedly alone."

"But what of Sister Willa's son?" I asked.

"That was not me. That was the natural death of a too-early child." Sister Willa looked relieved. She stepped back in acceptance. "I don't murder children. I just could not abide any more Gold Room wives."

"But wouldn't Willa have become a sealed, Gold Room wife?" I asked.

"That was at least a year away. A lot can happen in a year. And besides, she didn't annoy me like the others," she said dismissively.

White Cloud interrupted, "Who shot my father? Was that Mother Evangeline?"

"No," I said, "that was Brother Port trying to rile up the Shoshone."

Brother Port nodded without comment.

"I watched you grow." Mother Evangeline turned to the Patriarch and took up her tale. "I saw what use you tried to make of the missing pages that I had found and held. I watched your spurious Prophet-dom evolve like a spreading contagion. I watched as you mystified others in an attempt to rise to the Twelve and beyond.

CHAPTER SEVENTEEN

Ultimately, John Sweet, I watched because you amused me!" she exclaimed contemptuously.

"But is not the Patriarch a true Prophet?" I goaded her.

"He is a false husband, a false teacher, a false preacher, a false Prophet. I, most of all, knew how fraudulent you are. My murdering was commentary on your fraud." She turned to face John Sweet. "You wanted to be a member of the elect, an Apostle. If you be the Twelfth, John Sweet, then you are Judas!"

Brother Port gave a smile of satisfaction.

"What is this of the missing pages?" I asked Mother Evangeline directly.

"What missing pages?" She smiled at John Sweet. "There are no missing pages. They are lost like kindling in a fire. Even those that have been edited, scribbler. Kindling."

John Sweet fled to his study. He returned ashen.

"Gone," he said.

"What's gone?" Brother Port queried.

"The pages. No more," the Patriarch answered reluctantly.

"But what of our translation?" I asked quickly. Could it be that something I had edited was no more? The writer in me blanched.

"Nothing is left. There was the smell of a fire in the hearth. An August fire," the Patriarch said haltingly. He righted himself and faced Mother Evangeline. "Evangeline, what have you done with my Prophecy?"

"Prophecy?" she accused. "I have burned the inferior work my brother scribbled. I have rejected what you and this detecting editor have done to them. I have destroyed these fraudulent pages."

"But what of my Prophecy? What of Another Book?"

"Don't we Mormons have enough books, enough edicts, enough Prophecy?" she started to shout.

"But I am a true Prophet."

"John Sweet, nothing you do contains either truth or Prophecy!"

The Patriarch raised himself to his full height and faced Mother Evangeline. "You are not my wife and I am not your husband."

Evangeline cast him a bitter smile. "Then I can go wherever God sends me safely alone. I accept fully the sin of murder for which there is no forgiveness. In killing I have given up all hope of salvation. Hewn down, I will yet be cast into the fire. I will be filthy. But I feared more the straight gate of Celestial Marriage. I chose to forego exaltation and to suffer in my pride separately and singly."

She paused and then turned to me, the detective. "I will not commit suicide to close neatly this story. I have chosen the plot line, and I will watch the play's finish with full engagement."

Brother Port took Evangeline's hand. "I will bring you to the Golden City. I will take you to Brother Brigham. He will give verdict. It is not for John Sweet, this failed, fraudulent Prophet to decide your fate. He has not tended to his family so others must." He led her away.

John Sweet, shorn of his book and all of his Gold Room wives, looked smaller to me. Torn of his mantle of righteousness, he was no longer a Prophet. He was alone.

AUGUST 3, 1862
SWEETVILLE

I had sought something from this Patriarch, something I did not

CHAPTER SEVENTEEN

find. I sought a Father, a Patriarch. I, as a son, tried to be worthy of this Father as his scribe. I edited what was given to me to the best of my abilities. I sought a book to craft and to believe in. All I found was a pseudo-Prophet, a phantom Father, and a spurious book that did not survive.

I was given two riddles in this tale. The Sisters' deaths. What I was to become.

I, who had lost a wife I no longer wanted, had searched for some new reason to continue on. I had spent more energy in this search than mere detecting. I had failed in this search. Alone I must look elsewhere for future solace.

At least, at last, I had rallied to tidy up, to find closure in detection.

Crime engendered, its murders, and its aftermath are one story. The strongest faith may yet become madness. Mother Evangeline committed these crimes fully knowing what her final penalty would be. She was at peace with her lot, for it guaranteed her freedom in an afterlife without Patriarchs.

After the murderess had been taken away, three of the wives from the Blue Room stayed close to each other. None looked to the Patriarch. Sister Katherine, not far from death, pondered her decision for polygamy. Sister Nona hunkered down with the inner demons of her choice. Sister Willa, son-less but complete in her usefulness, led the three from the room.

Chief Sagwitch, Evan, White Cloud—for there was no more Sister Sarah—and Twin Spirit remained in one grouping far from the fading Patriarch. White Cloud spoke up in Shoshone, "Come, Tekwahi. Lead us to our rightful place." Evan smiled as he prepared to go.

Twin Spirit, this apron-wearing man, this bravest of the brave, this ultimate truth teller, turned to me. "Be well, Eugene. I do not need to call you a brother for we are brothers in deed." He faced me and the others, excluding John Sweet, who of course was not listening. "We must be hurt in order to heal, and then go onward."

Made in the USA
Middletown, DE
22 September 2019